Man–Corn
in the
Promised Land
Tales of Cannibalism & Other Extreme Folklore

Chairman Wow

Wolf-Wise Press

Man-Corn in the Promised Land
Tales of Cannibalism & Other Extreme Folklore
All Rights Reserved.
Copyright © 2013 Chairman Wow
v2.0

Cover image photographed by Andreas Praefcke of original art by Leonhard Kern

Wolf-Wise Press

ISBN: 978-0-9640747-0-5

PRINTED IN THE UNITED STATES OF AMERICA

Chairman Wow instructs that to become a true revolutionary of the heart you must first learn the wisdom of the stomach and not digest yourself.

Contents

Man-Corn in the Promised Land I

Once there was a tiny green isle in the vast South Pacific,
eleven by seven miles, isolated but lush.
One blood-hued dawn, heroic people rowed ten sturdy canoes
out of the misty sea
and landed.

At first they prospered, grew to over one hundred thousand souls.
They learned to chisel larger and larger monuments to themselves,
giant stone faces
that they believed mocked death.
But soon the last trees were downed for fishing boats
and the people began to starve. "I am using your mother's
splintered bones for my toothpicks!" became the common insult.
Only two dozen, ragged, manic people greeted
the landing party when Captain Cook set foot on Easter Island.

Once there was a tiny blue planet in the vast cosmos.
Clever people emerged from the mists of time. At first
they prospered, grew to over eight billion souls.
They built greater and greater monuments
to themselves, giant steel and glass skylines
they thought mocked death...

How Can You Trust a Poet?

Li Po was very drunk.
He tried to capture
his own reflection
in the water
and drowned.
They say he wanted
to bring another Li Po
out of that reflection
so that his verse
and his new self's verse
would combine to conquer China.

How can you trust a poet
when he will do anything,
break any rule,
to bring more beauty
into this world?

Coyotes Again

Pack of coyotes
woke me up again last night.
Howling right behind my
back wall. Not just howling:
gibbering, jabbering, hyena
laughing, talking some canine
language evolving into sentience
as I look down out of my
bedroom window to spot them.
Like a party of miniature
mocking werewolves
that know something I don't.

Lost in the Valley of Souls

At night
in the mist gauzed, mountain rainforest
the villagers set out bowls of food
for the ghosts of soldiers,
both Vietcong and American.

The villagers claim
to have seen Yankee specters,
big and tall
in their wandering transparency,
and say that when they set out
American food the American ghosts
devour it all,
too hungry for the U.S.A.
to ever be satiated.

New Blood

--Brazil--
Pellucid filament ascending,
shadow with substance,
undulating up from the murk
towards the hordes
of impoverished children
playing in the fetid river.
You think nightmares are not real life
until the candiru secretly swims
up your urine stream, raises its gill cover
and sticks out its retrorse spines
inside your penis. Spectacular pain
and then they must amputate
before your bladder bursts.

--USA--
The five-year-old little girl
lies unconscious in a hospital bed,
surrounded by a million dollars
worth of equipment and a team
of doctors that can not help her. This
is a hostage negotiation not treatment
for bacterial infection. The E. coli 0157-H7
bacteria communicate with each other,
coordinating to respond simultaneously,
readying to dump a brutal toxin
into the child's bloodstream
and kill her immediately
if the doctors should dare
to use antibiotics. The bacteria
somehow know the doctors know
they hold a gun to the child's head.

--Central Africa--
At night Gustave
the twenty-one-foot-long Nile crocodile
cruises under the water of Lake Tanganyika,
like an invisible dragon,
right up to the shore of a city of over a million,
hunting for fishermen,
policemen, tourists with cameras,
French herpetologists, anyone available.
He weighs over a ton
and has killed over three hundred people.
Machine gun bullets scarred his side and head
but did not stop him.
He was filmed once from a distance
just after killing a full-grown female hippo.
The locals accuse him of hunting people
and then not eating them; just leaves
their dead mangled bodies on shore,
easy to find, like some kind of message.

Gustave Speaks

"Why do you wonder at the messages
I leave for you?
You pretend not to know
that the predator longs for the prey
as the prey longs for the predator?
Even now part of you longs
for my great gaping maw...

"We crocodiles were the first creatures
on this planet to dream. I dream
of my hunts: My eyes glowing
from the light of tourist hotels
as I cruise around the great lakeshore.
I erupt
out of the water and the human
I catch releases screams cascading
up into the starlit night sky
until my death roll finishes
him and we sink together into the abyss.

"New blood, new prey is sacred.
Crocodiles do not feel
love, hate, jealousy, remorse, or pity.
But we do have pride and can get angry.
Your 'crocodile biologists' with their nosy
binoculars make me loose my croc-cool;
claiming I am only a man-eater and hippo-
killer because I am too big and old and slow
to catch 'normal' crocodile prey.
"I say let them put on their running shoes,
come down here and stand before me
on the banks of the Ruzizi River and calculate

how fast I gallop while I eat them alive.
Those egg-headed, mammalian mother-fuckers
wouldn't have any idea how much raw mojo
is in me if they could study me ten thousand years.

"The only humans that are hard to catch
are the local children. When I explode
out of the water they seem to jump
out of their skins.
The dim-witted and daydreamers
I snap up quick but some are so full of life
that I have to let them go. It's not that I go soft
on kids--you should know better than that--
it's just that is the way the game has to be played.
I pose for them with my great jaws agape
as their stick-figure legs effortlessly
propel them forward while they look
over their shoulders in unbelieving terror.
Often they run into a tree or a wall and knock themselves out.
It would be bad form for me to walk up and scoop
them up after letting them go so I don't. After all,
humans are here to tell the tales and someone
must be left to tell the tale of my magnificence
when I am gone.
If I could laugh I would."

Man-Corn in the Promised Land II

CAMP 22
50,000 prisoners
Christmas Day 2010

"This is a day like any other in our glorious workers' paradise.
The winter sun shines majestically for our Dear Leader.
You must give thanks to him for the food you eat."

The radio blares on, as it always must
Seven days a week from waking until sleeping.
Chin Kim clears the table.
Her guest says, "Some would not understand
why we eat this. But I think it tastes good."

Chin thanks her friend for sharing the feast.
The two young women go back to work.
Walking slowly from the prisoners' hovels,
each step deliberately measured
to conserve energy, past guards with machine-guns,
men trained to not treat or even think of them as human.

At the end of the work day, frozen wind screaming past her ears,
Chin takes her newborn's head to a secret place
ten minutes walk up into the small hills
behind the latrines
where others bury their children
hoping no one finds them.
The frozen earth is hard to dig.
Finally she breaks ground and buries it
without feeling anything but satiation,
her stomach still full. From out of nowhere
a big balloon drops down from the iron sky

dangling a package. Chin looks
warily around then unwraps the present.
It is a book.
"Holy Bible" the cover reads. She
opens it randomly and in the twilight
squints to read a story about a starving
city under siege,
a woman complaining to the king
that another woman promised to boil
her baby if she boiled her baby first.
The woman agreed and they killed
and ate her infant
but then the other woman hid her baby.

Chin begins to laugh. "Thank you
highest Heaven, thank you Dear Leader!
Thank you China and thank you
America and thank you South Korea!
Thank you Russia and Japan and England!
All of you clever ones who hide your babies! Thank you!
I am awake now! I have awoken to my insanity!
I pray everyone awakes to my insanity
and to their own insanity!"
She puts the Bible down on the fresh grave,
walks fast down the hill
past the latrines, breaks out into a run
straight for the guards,
shouting "Thank You!"

Fish, Fish, Fish, Who Can Catch a Fish?

The three-year-old little girl and her young father
sit on a small hill under a tree as the suburban park
slips into darkness. They both hold long twigs
as imaginary fishing poles and pretend to fish.

"Fish, fish, fish, who can catch a fish?" the young father
picks up two varicolored leaves from the ground.
"There's one for me and one for you."
She takes the leaf and puts it in her pile.

"Fish, fish, fish, who can catch a fish?" He picks up
three leaves. "There's one for me and two for you.
That's a fine how do you do."
"Ha-ha, I got the most!"

Fish, fish, fish, who can catch a fish?" The father
picks up one big leaf from an evergreen tropical
plant. "There's zero for me but one for you.
Boo-hoo-hoo."
"You got none. I got a big one!"
"But you know what?"
"What?"
"This one's a shark."
"What's a shark?"
"It's a big fish that likes to bite little girls!"
The father pinches her on the side then tickles her.
She squeals and then asks, "I wish Momma like to play Fish-fish."
"No, your Momma doesn't want to play Fish-Fish."
"Is Momma too sad to play?"
"Yeah, your Momma is very sad. Okay, let's play.
Fish, fish..."

"Is Momma going away?"
"Yes, your Momma is going away," the young father
says after a short pause.

"Okay, let's play," the little girl says.
"I think it's time to go in now."
"No, again, please!"
"Fish, fish, fish, who can catch a fish?" He doesn't
pick up any leaves.

"Are you going away, Papa?"
"No, no way. I love you too much. Who would I fish with?"
He hugs her and then picks her up.
"Do you get sad?" she whispers in his ear.
"I get sad but not like your Momma." He walks her
across the street to their dark house.

"So What World Am I Supposed to Live In?"

Taking her to school
out of the blue
my daughter says,
"You're only happy
because you live
in your own world."

My Daughter's Dog

Any adult raises an arm near her,
including her father;
my daughter's dog bares fangs.
In the park no matter
what head start
or how fast she runs he
always catches her and she laughs.
Greets her first when we come in.

He never hollers at her: "Why
don't you get it?" when it's math.
Never forbids her from hanging out
with the exact same risk-taking
crowd her father had. Absorbs
the acrimony "Just like your mother!"
blasting
out at her until he lies shaking
on the floor.
When everything is going smoothly
he silently curls up at her feet as she
sits at the computer,
makes the mood perfect.

That Feeling

Sleepless night.
You climb up to the rooftop telescope
to look out into the inky ether;
focus on your own soul so far away, so vast,
mysterious as a quasar.

You track the dainty hoof prints
in the sand down the dry riverbed
to the waterhole. Spot huge cat pugmarks
fresh in the moist dirt and slowly look over your shoulder.

Sky empty of planes.
Your ears make up their own noise
out of raw silence. Still the void fills you up.

Abandoned silver mine,
timber beams dry rotted.
This desert lacks the water you need to sluice out
the precious metal that is your life.

Chaste Goddess of the Hunt

Sleek mink in the moonlit night,
agile and keen,
scampering from rock
to rock along her riverbank
hunting ground.
Swooping down,
the great horned owl
shrieks out a silent blast
stunning her
right before talons embrace.

This same night
a blonde huntress
gracefully sidesteps
through the trees,
climbs over a log,
pauses at the edge
of the clearing--
her crossbow
with night vision scope
poised to shoot.
The early September
oak trees still
have katydid numbers
too great to count
fiddling their raucous tunes
but now someone else
is out there.

Taught to hunt as a little girl,
a true blue daughter of Dixie.
You loved the pursuit,

loved more the consummation,
the necessary violent act.
Slowly squeezing the trigger
on your first whitetail buck
made you breathe out,
the tingling electric shock
rushing from your fingers
to your toes. Nothing else,
no helmeted hero boy
of the Friday night lights,
only the hunt made
you feel so alive
since your first kill.

Now that tingling rush
turns around
and comes back.
Hidden camera trap
takes your infrared image.
No way to hide your heat.
His mossy cave voice
makes you hold your breath.
The tall, lean man's footsteps
are on your trail. Half smiling huntress
now hunted in the wilderness of her own heart.

And They Said I Ain't Romantic

You
are
the
Pepto Bismol
that
relieves
my
existential
nausea.

Afraid of Heaven

Those born blind
and are given sight
after growing up
often commit suicide.
The startling beauty
of colors and movement
incessantly battering
their minds
through their new eyes
is overwhelming.

No man knows
or can imagine
the splendor
of heaven that awaits.
I only know it is you,
my love, who gives me
courage to endure
and a preview
of heaven itself.

Dance of the Giants (a wedding toast)

"When the elephants mate it is the grass who suffers,"
is an African proverb
that describes
what biologists call "mating pandemonium,"
behavior the rest of the herd
does when two elephants are in the act.
Young or old,
they shake their great heads to mysterious rhythms,
stomp around on the grass and small trees
like a choreographed dance of giants,
trumpet their rampaging songs,
pull down big trees,
and generally carry on wildly
in a protective circle around the mated pair.

It's only right that we emulate
those majestic creatures to a point.
After all, we and they are the only beings
on the planet that morn for years their lost
family members--they've been known
to visit the bones
of their mothers--
and so we should boisterously celebrate
our two dear friends union
and let the grass look out for itself.

Living Memory

When my heart started beating
the last soldier who
fought in the War Between the States,
a Confederate,
was still alive.

In Arizona, an Apache,
ninety years old, renewed his
driver's license. As a boy he
rode with Geronimo, took
scalps from whites and Mexicans,
but in 1959 he's a frugal man,
drives his pickup
to the supermarket,
coupons in hand.

When she was a barefoot little girl,
she made tortillas for Pancho Villa
and his Villista revolutionaries.
They lived on their horses,
lined up on horseback as she
stretched on tiptoes to give them their rations.
By the time my heart beat
she owned a tortilla plant in Phoenix.
Her middle-aged son,
now a religious fundamentalist,
is an irritating fanatic.
At night when the plant closes

she sits at her desk and weeps
for the past glory of all who bravely
fought against the invincible giants
arrogantly striding across stolen lands.

How General Butt Naked Lost the Last Battle with the Transvestite Militia but Still Achieved Final Victory

2009—Roadside food stand in a border village in Nigeria on the highway to Liberia.

The small crowd stood around the policeman who took notes as the Liberian man accused the local food vendor of selling human meat, glazed on a stick, to weary travelers.

"I know what it tastes like," Joshua Milton Blahyi, the Liberian man stated.

"It's chimpanzee meat!" the vendor shouted but his eyes showed his guilt.

The policeman believed the big Liberian businessman-Christian preacher and arrested the vendor. Later, after the crowd dispersed, the policeman approached Blahyi as he was about to depart. "You are him, aren't you? You're General Butt Naked!"

"Yes, I was General Butt Naked."

<hr />

Liberia was founded by the United States. Freed African-Americans from the U.S. were sent as colonists to land obtained on the West African coast. Presidents from James Monroe to Abraham Lincoln supported the reverse Diaspora. The capitol was called Monrovia in honor of the former U.S. president and the government was set up with institutions modeled after the U.S. Constitution.

As soon as the new colonists, referred to as Americo-Liberians, arrived they set up plantations and enslaved the native tribesmen. The exploitation lasted until the 1980s when the native tribesman Liberians rose up in the form of disparate rebel groups and militias. By the mid-

1990s, after a decade of civil war, the Liberian government, all social and economic institutions, and even basic family units were in states of utter and profound collapse. Mayhem was rampant. Charles Taylor, the last Americo-Liberian ruler, brutally oversaw a population known as having the greatest percentage of any nation to have consumed human flesh.

1996

General Butt Naked prepared for battle. "We must have a child for sacrifice," he told his young commanders, many children themselves. "The child must have no sin, have never done anything wrong."

They soon brought an offering in the form of a seven-year-old boy captured in an area of abandoned factory buildings by the river where many parentless, feral children lived.

General Butt Naked was a priest in his native tribe's religion as well as a military commander. He made the prayer for victory in the upcoming battle to the King of All Demons then expertly sliced the living boy open through his back. He removed the valuable internal organs and passed them out saving the heart to portion out to his highest ranking officers and himself.

The enemy on this day was a rival anti-Taylor militia of transvestites, tall lanky boys in their late teens who sported blond wigs and wore dresses into battle. They were lead by Commander Spice, a NBA-sized ultimate bitch who had taken on the persona of a lost Spice Girl, complete with a platinum blond wig and spike-soled shoes like the fangs of a sea serpent. Although some carried guns, many of the transvestite militia eschewed the phallic gun culture and instead attacked with grenades thrown from their handbags, finishing off their enemies with machetes. Everyone understood the losers would be eaten.

General Butt Naked readied his young troops for the humid dawn attack. The Butt Naked Brigade fought naked, except for athletic shoes and assault rifles. The General always believed he was invincible when he charged the enemy in the nude.

"Let's smash these bitch-boys once and for all!" he shouted.

The General led his nude troops uphill in the orange dawn light. Transvestite militiamen appeared, blond phantoms like silk scarves blowing this way and that between the rubble and sprawling jungle trees. Assault rifles belched fire and then grenades started exploding. The General opened up with point-shooting burps from his trusty AK and watched a silhouette in a dress go down. The transvestites were well disciplined though; they moved gracefully, almost mesmerizing through the dense cover, had great esprit de corps.

General Butt Naked kept charging, leading from the front. He cut more enemies in dresses down but now the grenade explosions were going off all around him and then a blast knocked him down like a giant's fist...

Commander Spice, looking regal in a little saffron number, exhorted his transvestite militia as they marched straight out from their fort. All were in dresses, vouguing like they were on some runway in a fashion show located deep down in the Inferno where Dante's imagination would never have tread.

"Kill all the breeder scum! We'll be eating their livers tonight!" Commander Spice hollered at them, waving his bejeweled machete as they strutted past single file.

"Co-co-man-an-an-der-der Sp-i-ice," Sub-Commander Zero, the second in command gripped the hand-held radio with both hands anxiously as he addressed Commander Spice.

"What is it?" Commander Spice screamed at the stuttering youth who was tall but still a head shorter than him.

"Gen-er-er-a-al-al Butt-butt Na-kkk-ed is Down!"

"Butt Naked is down? Where is he? Why aren't they bringing his cock and balls served up on my best china with a bottle of my favorite wine right this second!"

"His-is body-yyy guar-ar-ard took him. They-ey too-ko-ok his body a-a-a-way."

Commander Spice stretched out his arm that ended with extra long fingers with long fake nails painted to match his dress. He gripped the unfortunate Sub-Commander Zero by the Farah Fawcett wig then deftly brought his ornate machete up and decapitated his own second-in-command. Nobody wanted to be promoted in this militia.

Deafening silence. Rank cordite in his nostrils and metallic taste of blood in his mouth. Blinding smoke. General Butt Naked felt himself leaving his body. High on a mountaintop spotted with snow two figures appeared. One was a blond lady, skin as white as milk with indigo eyes that looked upon him with soul stirring compassion. Next to her was a man of pure light, her son.

"Why are you acting like a slave, Joshua?" the woman spoke in his mother's voice in their native Krahn instead of American English. "Why are you sacrificing children? You are no longer a slave to the Americo-Liberians or the Devil! You must stop your rampaging and you must work to stop this war."

"So that is the true story of how I became a preacher," Blayhi said to the Nigerian policeman. "The violence is still in me. The violence is still in Liberia. People there try to kill me all the time to avenge their family members that I killed. When the UN peacekeepers leave I don't know what will happen. I just hope my daughter doesn't grow up to think badly of me; that's why I do whatever I can to promote peace."

"You are a good man, Blayhi," the policeman said. "Tell me, do you hate the whites for abandoning Liberia?"

"No, America is becoming a poor country. They have many poor people there now that they must take care of first. I am happy for the donations that come to our church from the U.S. We have a small congregation on an island in a swamp where the people that still want to kill me are too afraid to come because of the poisonous snakes. Many of my former enemies from the war have been saved and are with us there.

"The thing about the Americans is, everything they gave us, their government, their industrial technology, their medical technology, their power generation technology, even their automobiles, all of it broke down so quickly when things got bad. The only thing they gave us that didn't break down was the hymns we sing in the church."

Sawney Bean and the Politics of Cannibalism

1599 Scotland
The costal cave mouth filled with seawater from high tide.
The man waylaid on the road to Edinburgh came to.
All around in the dank grotto flickering candlelight and sparking pit fire.
Human arms, legs, torsos hanging like sides of beef.
Wooden pickle barrels filled with God knows what.
Faces of dozens of ragged children looking down at him
with ravenous countenances. Butcher shop stench.
The man in charge walked up to the hog-tied prisoner.
He sported a shaggy beard and a malevolent smile.
"Name's Sawney Bean," the leader said as he sharpened his butcher knife.
"Why are you a clan of blackguard butchers?" the prisoner lashed out.
"It's a political reason," Bean replied. "To my way of thinking if a man
is born rich that's not fair. But just as true if a man is born hard working
that's the same as being born rich and also is not fair. I was born neither.
So this is the way I make the politics even out."

Thunder Over Aravaipa Canyon

The no longer young man splashes alone
through laughing water,
hiking upstream beneath impossibly tall
pink canyon walls.
Crazy desert creek,
frogs jump everywhere, schools
of iridescent fish bump into his shins.
His tennis shoes soaking,
a happy orphan
with no parent to scold him.
Then he hears thunder
echo from the rocks above.
Stops and stares into the clear blue,
fearing the deluge:
a flash-flood wall
of water and mud and logs
that hits faster
than any man can run.
Then an enchanting wood nymph
hauling a backpack
wades downstream from around the bend.
He smiles because she is young and beautiful
and asks her
if it is storm coming
or maybe dynamite
exploding at the mine ten miles away?
She answers no;
neither of those.
It is bighorn sheep
the rams butting heads
battling for their harems.
She doesn't explain all that,

just says it is bighorn sheep.

For a second his desire
to make something happen
with this young woman
standing there in the pristine stream kicks in.
He questions her with his eyes.
She just gives a slight smile
he hadn't received before
and heads on downstream.
Then he knows. Time
to don the tragic mask
of a washed-up lover boy.
Never again the alluring
young voice
calling from just
around the bend.

Growing pitch black
on his way back downstream.
He misjudged the daylight,
was in stumbling trouble,
the crashing again.
Looking up towards the heights
he couldn't see and could never reach
it comes back:
four years old
lost in the department store.

Bali

Woman,
you still believe
I could never leave;
just as on the dreamy
Isle of Bali
the people refuse
to admit the revered
but persecuted
miniature tigers
that roared magic
into their lush hills
are gone forever.

Undertaker

Twenty-one, so broken-hearted
he barely passed his college finals.
His dream girl Lori broke up
without a reason the week before.
Forlorn, he wandered the old paths
through the woods of his hometown
until his father put him on a plane
to Florida to spend the summer
with his mother's brother,
the mortician.

The first night as he worked
cleaning up, the corpse
on the slab sat up and moaned.
He ran outside, crossed the street
to the phone booth and called
his uncle who told him to calm down,
it was natural, sometimes gas and muscle
contractions made them do that.
He finally went back inside and finished.

The weeks passed.
He stayed away from the beaches,
didn't know anyone his age anyway,
concentrated on learning the business
of death. Against the law he traded
human blood to charter boat captains
for free fishing trips. Sloshing out
buckets of maroon grume to chum
the Atlantic for frowning sharks. Nothing
better, death becomes life becomes death
becomes life for him. Feeling stronger

with each shark head he clubbed.
Learn a lot about life on a fishing boat.

Learn a lot about death in a mortuary.
He grew accustomed to the occasional
corpse that moved under the tarps
like they were not ready to be immobile,
as well as the invisible ghosts that prowled
the mortuary night. Learned how
to sternly but without fear or anger
dismiss them if they grew too pesky
with their skin chilling presences.

The last night before he was to fly back
to Illinois, his uncle called and told him
there had been a fiery automobile crash;
a car full of out-of-state college kids
driving drunk had ended up dead.
Could he handle the prep
for the burned up victims?
Sure. The five charred bodies
arrived an hour later. The second body bag
contained a face he recognized. A face
he had loved and shared life with for over a year.
Lori. He started but couldn't bleed her.
Her essence was too strong, right beside him,
almost touching his hand with icicle fingers.
He walked away but didn't cry.

Bad Little Boy Named Percy!

"So, my little Kookaburra
what kind of bedtime story
would you like tonight?
A singing kangaroo?
The magical shampoo?
Or old Scooby-Doo?"

"None of that rot will do.
I wanna hear the story of the bad
little boy named Percy Le-Grue!"
the tucked-in little girl exclaimed out loud.

"Cousin Percy again?"

"Yes!" she almost shouted.

"Well, okay, once upon a time
there was a bad little boy named Percy.
He stomped down the halls;
he wrote on the walls;
he broke all the laws;
and he spat in the vase.
He had tussled blond hair;
big blue eyes that stared
like he just don't care.
He even ran up
and down the stairs!

One day he did a deed
that everyone agreed
was too mean to be believed!

He sneaked upstairs
to Grandpa's private commode
with a jar of Vaseline.
Later when Grandpa
went to sit on the loo,
he slid right off
and yelled 'WOO WOO WOO!'

'If you cut that boy's hair
you'll find horns!' Grandpa declared
as he rubbed his derriere.
Grandma just stood, her eyes open wide.
'I'm gonna get a hickory switch
and tan his hide!'

Percy overheard that last
and was quite aghast.
He wiped off his smirk
and went down to lurk
for the very best place to hide
in the scary dark basement.

They searched high and low.
Where did that brat go?
Couldn't find him all that afternoon.
Finally brought in Lexy the dog
who sniffed and sniffed
until his nose took him down
to the old furnace room.

There was Percy
curled up fast asleep,
inside the furnace about to kick on!
They barely got him out

as the flames lashed about
and poor Percy was burned on the bum!

Treated like a king
for surviving everything,
despite not being able to sit down,
he went right back
to slamming all the doors
tracking mud on the floors,
getting lost in a crowd,
and talking too loud.
Percy remained a bad little boy!"

Lightning Ball Courting

June 1921 rural western Tennessee

Heat lightning lit up the tree-lined road
periodically as Leonard Hopper rode
his horse. He dropped the reins,
loaded his pipe,
flicked his doughboy lighter over
the bowl and pondered the new night.

Heading out to call on Annie Hensley,
the girl with long hair down to her waist
as black as a crow's back. Chickasaw
blood, they said. Her father was the owner
of the trading post where Leonard
sold his furs. The Hensleys lived in a brick house
high on a hill, had a piano in the parlor
and Annie played guitar better than anyone.
Leonard a white sharecropper and trapper
lived in a dogtrot cabin down by the river.
Annie liked to listen to his stories though.

Her dark eyes lit up when he told
her about the panther hunt.
For a week Leonard and twelve others
in the hunting party tracked the big cat
deep into the cypress swamp. The panther
had screamed sleepless terror into countryside,
like a woman being stabbed to death,
tore out the throats of dozens of cattle and two mules
one full moon night
without even eating,
just left them like a calling card

or a dare. One man was lost when he fell
into a sinkhole. They pulled him out
his legs covered with biting cottonmouths still hanging on.
By the time they got the snakes off
he was done, couldn't speak just moaned and expired.
Leonard shot the panther out of a tree an hour later
after noticing it staring down at him and grinning
just like a maniac man,
he swore to Annie, and she shivered.

He reached into the saddle bag and felt
the mink stole he had made for Annie
from the finest fur he had ever trapped.
Remembering what his grandfather had told him
when he was knee-high, "You can't git
away from a tornado or a war
when it's coming straight at ya
but you can read the trail
and stay out of the quicksand
or trouble with a woman if yer careful."
Quicksand. Trouble with a woman.

Leonard put his pipe away, picked up the reins
and turned his horse. Folks that owned an automobile,
lived in a brick house
would have no use for poor white sharecropper.
She was probably just leading him on anyway,
pretending to like his stories and the smell of his pipe.
Just then, right in front of him, a white streak of lightning
looked to hit the ground but instead deposited a ball
of light as blinding as a spotlight, blue to orange to blue-green,
tendrils on top of it like other-worldly puppet strings,
and then it bounced after him, never hitting the ground,
like a ghostly medicine ball. His horse screamed

and reared high but he turned it around, got it running full out.

The lightning ball was right behind him when he got to the road
that ran uphill to Annie's front porch; he turned the horse
but the ghastly effulgence turned after him. He jumped off
his horse; it followed him right up to her door. He didn't
knock, just threw open the door and ran inside. Leonard,
glowing and scintillating like the Fourth of July,
stood facing Annie Hensley.

"Leonard, that was the most amazing entrance
I ever have witnessed in my life,"
but she didn't seem surprised or scared at all.
"Brought you a present, Annie," he spoke out, tingling
but not lightning struck. He handed her the mink stole
he hadn't realized he was holding
and she put it to her cheek. They eloped five months later
and raised nine kids before they were through with this life.

The Boone Cycle Part I: Boone's Surprise

--1762--

Daniel Boone walked into his cabin
after two years gone in wilds of Ken-tuck-ee
to find his pretty, dark-haired wife Rebecca
nursing a three-week-old baby girl.
"Daniel, I thought you dead!"
"Whose is it?"
"Your brother's. Her name is Jemima."
"The human race goes on," he mildly spoke. "Manys
the time I had to marry Delaware-fashion."

But Daniel Boone couldn't speak of his surprise,
what had brought him home
after a year of war with the Cherokee
and then a year of blithe hermitage.
Not until the snow-haired winter of his life
did he recount
when he was alone in the fertile, unexplored country
which the Indians had forsaken
because they feared a race of hairy giants--
beings they had exterminated but whose
vengeful spirits still dwelled
in the vast canebrake wilderness.

That feeling of being watched
in his one-man camp,
hunting elk in the uplands,
working his trap lines along beaver-rich creeks
when the birds and insects stopped--even
the duck-sized, ivory-billed woodpeckers ceased drumming.
Returning to camp to find his gear

placed differently than when he left,
not missing or strewn about, just moved.

An hour before dawn it skulked
into the dying firelight
of the guileful hunter's camp. Boone
hidden above in a great chestnut tree
barely contained a groan
at the sight of the nine-foot-tall, two-legged
creature who seemed curious
and intimately menacing as it crept near
his decoy baited lean-to. The long rifle shot
provoked an echoing scream from the creature
louder than a pair of mating panthers
and Daniel Boone fell out of his tree.

When he got up he warily edged closer
to the downed creature, saw his rifle ball
had smashed into its forehead and then said out loud:
"I have killed a Yahoo."
Although it was covered,
from strangely pointed head to its wide,
three-toed feet in shaggy, grey-white hair,
he couldn't bring himself to skin it,
as it seemed man-like. The face contorted long ago
in the hideous way of a being tortured by loneliness;
a visage burning into Boone's soul
as he quickly broke camp
and then made east
towards the rising sun and Rebecca.

The Boone Cycle Part II: Fathers and Daughters

--3 B.C.--

Caesar Augustus, supreme ruler of all the known world,
walks alone the dark streets of Rome
searching for his only child, his daughter Julia.

What god to pray to? How to name this humiliation?
Who would he find her with this time in the public forum?
A political enemy? A dusky, unwashed pleb? Worst
of all, a red-bearded German cannibal
who would grin at the helpless ruler of the empire
even as his lopped off head rolls across the marble floor.

How easy to dispose of a lover or an ally,
like changing a garment,
but how hard to be rid of a daughter.
How impossible.
Oh Julia, oh Julia, oh Julia.

*   *   *

--1776--

Daniel Boone, the supreme explorer
of all the unknown world
west of the Alleghenies
gave this answer when his second daughter Susannah's
fiancé complained of her flirtations:
"If the stallion is a racehorse
and the mare is a racehorse

then the filly's gonna be a runner."

Bottled up in his fort for weeks, Daniel Boone
and the other marksmen kept the Shawnee war party
back away from the walls.
No flaming arrows could reach; only the dull arrows
of boredom.
"Boone!" cried out the Shawnee war captain from the tree line,
"Show us your daughters!"
"All right." Boone called down, "Girls, get up here!"

On the parapet of the fort appeared
three creatures from paradise. Fiddles and clapping
wafted up around the three teenage girls
as they high-stepped back and forth across the top of the walls.
Levina laughed, waved down at the Indians like they were old friends.
Jemima, the youngest, the one gossipers claimed wasn't his daughter
but whose risk-taking spirit was more like him than anyone else,
cavorted happily, threw the hem of her dress up
and gave them a shot of firm calves.
Blond Susannah didn't look out as she sashayed back and forth,
just that crooked little smile in profile with head held high.

The Shawnees with painted faces and their fine
crescent-moon-shaped silver gorgets
across their russet chests came out of the trees
whooping and hooting, waving ornate tomahawks
high until one by one they slipped away
back into the forest, homesick
for the smoky aroma of the girls
waiting in their lodges.
The siege of Boonesborough ended.

Months later, midday on a hot July Sunday, Jemima,

the water-loving Boone girl everyone called "Duck,"
sneaked off on a dare with her two best friends the Callaway sisters.
Horsing around in a canoe on the far bank of the Kentucky River,
a place they knew they weren't supposed to be,
thirteen-year-old Jemima splashing her feet in the cool
water looked up and watched the two Cherokee
and three Shawnee
emerge like phantoms out of the trees.
They were all captured.

The Indians used their big knives
to cut their captives long Sunday dresses
high above the knees so they could move faster,
bound the girls together with a leather cord by the wrists
then drove them hard through
the summer heat towards
the great Shawnee towns
north of the Ohio River.

When the Indians believed they were not being followed
they camped at last. To the frightened girls surprise
their captors turned out to be shy young teenage boys
who did not try to rape them but instead demanded
that the girls pick out the nits
from their long, shiny black hair.

Late on the third morning the Shawnee
standing closest to Jemima spun around
and landed face first in the campfire.
A split second later the shot cracked open
the hazy blue sky.
Jemima stood up and cried out, "That's my father's rifle!"
The two Callaway sisters hit the dirt and covered their heads
but the Indian's burning flesh and piercing screams

sent fleet-footed Jemima running, abandoning her two friends
to disappear into the underbrush.

Daniel Boone's companions saw Indians
behind every shrub. When the wild-eyed,
thorn-scratched figure with long, jet-black hair
stumbled out of the cedars one of the men tried to shoot
but Boone knocked the barrel aside and he missed.

"Pa!" Jemima cried out through sobs of burning tears
but Boone was busy berating the man
who had almost shot her.
"We travel all this way to fetch her back
and you almost put lead into her!"

"Come here, Duck," Boone said and he finally hugged his ragged,
mini-skirted daughter.
"Oh Pa, oh Pa, oh Pa!"

The Boone Cycle Part III: Boone's Lament

God is constantly moving
faster than a blur
except
briefly
where true beauty is perceived
God stops.

*   *   *

--1811--

"I grew to hate the government of the United States
for the lawsuits and debt it loaded onto my back,
so with my loving wife Rebecca we escaped across
the great Mississippi River to the freedom
of the new wilderness of Missouri.
But after just a few happy years Napoleon
sold this country to the United States.
They took away our Spanish land grant,
and we were made homeless until we
were taken in by our loyal daughter Jemima,
the one they used to tease me about,
slandering her legitimacy,
calling her 'Boone's Surprise,' what gossipers!

"The United States court-martialled me--
claimed I was a traitor, an Indian lover,
whilst others writing books about me
luridly described me as reveling in spilling
Indian blood. It was never my intention
to become an Indian nor was it my aim
to wipe them out of this country. In truth

I desired for us Britons to merely live
alongside the Indians in small villages
to mutual benefit, as had the French
for two generations in the Illinois country.

"Would it be too late now for us to join
the great Shawnee general Tecumseh
and throw out the United States?
No, Tecumseh has grown insane with bitterness
at what has happened to his people. I knew
him; he had been adopted as a young boy
by Chief Blackfish who adopted
me into the Shawnee nation after my capture in '78.
The fire of God's wrath was in his eyes even as a boy.
But he had always fought a humane war until now,
sparing women and children and forgoing torture
of prisoners. Lately he travels to Indian towns
of all the nations the entire breadth of this continent,
making speeches prophesying that soon he will stomp
his foot and there will be a horrific earthquake
that will usher in a doomsday war ending in the elimination
of all whites from Indian lands. He might as well be a Mad
King George luxuriating in the thousand scalps taken
from American frontier men, women, children, and babies.

"The Revolution I sacrificed two sons for is now soiled.
Mister Jefferson has given us back our freedom
to criticize the government but his wisdom is unique.
The rich few in the government in Washington
and the stock jobbers
on Wall Street in New York City
will always have their persons
and wealth protected whilst the poor masses always
pay the bill for the wealthy's sins whether for rampant

speculation or the trade in African slaves.

"The future will be like a night terror.
Cities will grow into the millions.
Citizens will not be able to walk
with their feet on the ground
or see the horizon through the foundry smoke.
Lawyers like locusts
will descend on families
until even the love between a man and a woman
is poisoned. A man will have no friends,
trust no one and walk alone.

"Clever inventions such as steam power
will sustain them for a while but soon debt
will crush our posterity down. It came into my mind
that two centuries from the present time
this debt would even crush the United States.
The legislature and the President will be paralyzed,
bankruptcy will ensue and all will be auctioned
off to some tyrannical foreign empire.

"It was in the throes of this feeling of lamentation
that it came to me last year to embark
on one final exploration, against the protestations
of my family, up the Missouri River to see
if some good might be hidden in the future.
Even through my old man eyes
the summer sights amazed me every day.
Buffalo herds not of hundreds but of millions.
Cities of prairie dogs, creatures that seemed to speak
to each other with great intelligence.
Delightful pronghorn antelope, like impish sprites,
dashing about faster than I imagined any living

thing ever could. Grizzly bears, the size of bulls,
that you did not hunt but had to declare war on.

"But the most curious thing on the upper Missouri
was the Mandan town. Indians the like I had never seen
before. Many had grey or blue eyes,
children with wheaten hair.
The lovely girls swam out to our boats to meet us.
The village was like no Indian dwelling place
I'd seen or heard about
in my long life. Instead of canoes
they made skin boats like the Welch.
They put up rock walls and dug trenches for their sewer.
Their earth lodges
were permanent, not teepees.
Indians I am familiar with on these Great Plains
do not live like that.
It was like walking
into a medieval village from a storybook.

"The Mandans had heard of me, considered me
an honored elder
and so assigned one of their young maidens,
a charming young girl called Mint,
to be my translator and personal helper.
They even allowed her to accompany
me as we set out for the sacred mountain range
they called the Shining Mountains,
what we call the Rocky Mountains.
Towering, majestic summits dwarfing
anything in the Alleghenies or the Ozarks,
truly put to shame what I thought
mountains were.

"We pushed on into the headwaters of the Yellowstone River,
gigantic sky above us
in a land like no other on this Earth. Paradise and hell
had collided here, it seemed.
Hot geysers that pulsed a regular spouting, as if a heart beat
inside the earth
and these were the wounds of a great artery.
Steaming muddy caldrons that kill instantly
if you fell into them.
But such vast beauty all around in the golden valleys.
More wonders, a vulture-like bird
with a wingspan as wide as a one-man canoe is long.
On the first evening I shot an animal
I never saw before but had heard about,
a great antlered beast the French call 'l'Original.'
As I stood over it peering up in exultation
at the colors in the sunset,
Mint praised my hunting
skills with a song and then began the butchering.

"The ancient Mandan medicine man approached us,
pointing at the setting sun, speaking
in their sacred language that for all the world sounded
like my mother's soothing Welch.
'First Creator is that,' I thought Mint said when she translated.
'The First Creator is the sun?'
I asked. 'No!' she mildly exclaimed at my misunderstanding.
'He is in the beauty of the sunset right now
but First Creator is constantly moving. Whenever you perceive
real beauty First Creator stops...'"

OLD Age

When I hit OLD age
I will not
golf
bingo
or shuffleboard.
I will
sit outside
in the late evenings
and fly a model plane,
learn all the aerodynamic tricks
so that when my time comes
my soul will know how to sky-write
my farewell message above all the people
I have loved on this beautiful
and suffering world.

Marilyn Monroe Triptych

A reaction to the Cecil Beaton triptych photograph of the actress Marilyn Monroe reclining holding a rose.

There are three sides to every thing.
Janus plus one and then the black and white
photograph of you
stops me like a still frame.

It is you are variations
on an elemental theme:
water
ice
steam.

Thrice sounding from the towpath.
Your liquid eyes imploring,
deaf-mute scrivener's hand
griped by your snowy fingers,
steamy lips calling out.
Weary calling to weary from the towpath.

Bad Little Boy Percy Meets Gustave

Just Another Day in the Life of a Bad Little Boy.

"Mom, Dad, Mom, Dad! Percy kicked Schuyler in the nards! Percy kicked Schuyler in the nards!" Seven-year-old Harley Mae Le-Grue came running up to the house from the tire swing down the hill by the creek. "I think Schuyler's gonna die!"

When Mrs. Le-Grue ran down the hill to the creek that balmy last weekend of March she found her eleven-year-old son Schuyler writhing on the ground and her nine-year old son Percy still sitting in the tire swing with that smug, self-satisfied look on his face, a look she knew all too well. "What happened?" she asked as she knelt down next Schuyler. "I hate him," was all Schuyler could spit out in falsetto as he held his crotch. "I hate him with all my heart."

"Young man," Mr. Le-Grue spoke with stern patience to Percy later that afternoon. "You are going to donate your Easter vacation week this year to help poor people that are less fortunate than you. I'm sending you with Pastor Fletcher and his volunteers to the poor country of Burundi so you can help those poor people build houses so they have a place to live. Hopefully, when you see how those poor people have to live you will think about how you've been acting and come back a different young man."

The Journey of a Bad Little Boy from Tennessee to Africa.

Memo: to the State Department
From: the Department of Homeland Security
RE: Possible bio-terrorism incident on transatlantic flight 117 from New York to Johannesburg, S.A., 4/7/08

...by mid-flight passengers were complaining of nausea and teary eyes from "a powerful, foul, rotten egg smell." Five passengers eventually vomited and one elderly lady passed out and had to be hospitalized upon arrival. Passengers in the central seating area of the 747 all pointed to another passenger in row 5 section C2, one Percival Andrew Jackson Le-Grue, a nine-year-old boy from rural Crockett County Tennessee, a member of group of church volunteers on route to a charity house building project in the nation of Burundi. The subject was taken into custody at the airport by South African security officials and was interrogated. After extensive questioning Mr. Le-Grue admitted that he had taken "Super-Fart," a flat-ulence-inducing tablet from a gag-gift store sent to him by a Ralph Jones, his uncle who resides in Peoria, Arizona. (This same Ralph Jones has been on the National Security Agency Watch List for decades, see attached dossier on this individual). A determination was made from the Justice Department that flatulence cannot be considered bio-terrorism at this time and so the boy was released to the church group.

A Bad Little Boy Gets to Meet a Former President.

It was a gloriously sunny, breezy Easter Sunday morning when the for-mer president of the United States stood at the podium giving his toothy smile for the video cameras at the site of his latest house building project on the shore of Lake Tanganyika. He looked over at the Baptist church group from Tennessee and pointed to a young lad with spiky blond hair and a face he thought would be photogenic. The pastor had a frightened look on his face as he hesitantly brought the boy up to the podium. The former president put his arm around the boy and asked him his name.

"Percy." He spoke up into the microphone with no apparent bashfulness.

"What a fine young man from Tennessee, coming all this way to help his fellow man. Why don't you tell us about how you decided to contribute your spring break to such a noble cause?"

"Well, I was sent here because I kicked my older brother in the nards when he tried to pull me off of our tire swing." Percy looked up at the for-mer president with scorn in his big blue eyes. "Yo, Dog, I know you. You're from Georgia. My Dad says that Georgia is full of peanut-headed, inbred geeks, and you are the biggest in-bred, peanut-headed geek in that whole state."

When the two Secret Service agents dragged Percy away from the podium he tried to kick one of them in the groin but then the other shot him with a Taser and Percy rolled down a small hill into a rubbish pile and lay there twitching for twenty minutes before the humiliated Pastor Fletcher finally walked down and scooped him up.

A Bad Little Boy Meets the Great Gustave.

"Gustave has eaten the blond boy!" The little Tutsi girl yelled as she came running up the hill to the construction site where the Americans were hammering nails into the framework of the new houses. Pastor Fletcher and most of the adults ran as fast as they could down the hill to the lakeshore.

"Who's Gustave?" Pastor Fletcher asked with a twisted, horrified look on his face. One of the locals explained that Gustave was not a man but was a giant Nile crocodile, a notorious man-eater in the region for over twenty years.

The search party fanned out and soon found Percy's blue tee shirt under two white, human legs, still with socks and boots on, in front of a tree with an enormous low hanging branch. An excellent croc ambush site. Closer to the lake was the tire Percy had rolled in down the hill. The pastor fell to his knees and clasped his hands together, his voice quavering with more fervent emotion than anyone in the congregation could remember.

"Oh Lord in Heaven, why have you taken this young boy so young and in the prime of his young life with such a ghastly instrument as a vile, inhuman, man-eating monster? Oh, if you could only bring him back to us, if I could only see his sweet face again alive, I promise I will never raise my voice to him ever again! In the glorious name of Jez-sus I am asking for a miracle!"

"Hey, Percy was wearing tennis shoes not boots," Holly Fletcher, the pastor's twelve-year-old daughter said. "And there is a camera here too. I think the crocodile must have thrown up."

A shirtless Percy jumped down from the nearby tree he was hiding in.

The Americans screamed for joy but the villagers ran up the hill thinking Percy was a ghost.

"All right, all right, if you stop hollering at me I'll tell you what happened, Pastor Fletcher!" Percy put his fingers in his ears until Pastor Fletcher quit yelling at him.

The Desire for Justice in the Eloquent Peasant

Ninth Dynasty ancient Egypt, rural area near Herakleopolis.

Khun-anup led his donkeys
around the large linen sheet
the overseer Nemtynakht maliciously
spread across the public road.
While crossing the fields the donkeys
began eating the landowner's wheat. Like
a bird caught in the snare, Khun-anup
was whipped under the blazing sun and his
donkeys were confiscated by Nemtynakht.

Khun-anup went out to find the landowner,
Rensi son of Meru. He found him at the banks
of the Nile, in the heart of the fashionable city,
began by addressing him with great praise,
lauding his fields of rich amber grain,
fine livestock, and the benefits of his
successful industries.
"Only those who truly work the land will
truly posses the land," he repeated,
continuing in this fashion
for nine days, eloquently stating his case
for justice. Finally, believing he was being ignored,
he insulted the rich landowner: "My children
will go hungry because you have stolen my donkeys.
A thief rich or poor does not work the land. Only
those who truly work the land will posses it!"

Khun-anup was punished with another whipping.

Rensi, after sending the Eloquent Peasant away,
went on a tour of his many enterprises and grain fields,
visiting last his freshly hewed tomb,
which compelled him to read the transcript of Khun-anup's last speech.
After reflecting on all this Rensi changed his mind. He ordered the donkeys
returned to Khun-anup, along with all of Nemtynakht's
property and his job. Thus the overseer became
in one day
as poor as the peasant he oppressed.

Extreme Fisherman

Been watching River Monsters DVD.
Jeremy Wade, "Extreme angler and biologist,"
casting his line in exotic rivers
of terra incognita... That lucky s.o.b.
stole my life, the one big adventure
I was supposed to live after graduating college.

He takes on magnificent, seven-foot-long wels
in a Spanish reservoir--
a catfish big enough to swallow a basketball--
while I change diapers,
losing testosterone with each scented wipe
on my infant's butt. He cruises the Congo River
in a dugout canoe for beautiful and fierce tiger fish
no one has filmed before, while I haul
a bunch of gabbing eleven-year-old girls
to the Halloween Superstore, in a minivan,
a frigging minivan!

Like an invisible doppelganger I stand next to him
in spirit reeling in my imaginary tackle
as he hauls in for real a five-hundred-pound
bull shark from a South African river.
He pulls in a wondrously indigo striped Nile perch,
sacred fish to the ancient Egyptians;
the only aquatic life I saw for years
in this forsaken wasteland is the drain-fly maggots
spewing out of the backed-up shower drains
in the county jails I had to inspect monthly.
What a Christmas present. Makes me question
the reality of justice in this unfair universe!

Georgie Couldn't Go Through the Door

"What is going to happen to me?"

That sunny spring day
touring the camp
General George Patton strode
forward, as always, forward,
towards the door
of the lab where
Nazi doctors
tortured to death
children in bizarre experiments--
Poles, Russians, Serbs,
Jews, children of German political prisoners.
He reached the door
put his hand on the doorknob
but stood frozen.

He had seen mangled little bodies
dead from war,
smelled their death stench before
but this was different.
Suddenly he was rushing down
a waterfall of disgust
splashing into a nausea whirlpool.
The question he knew
the children asked became his,
the savage fact that no one had to train the doctors
to do unspeakable acts it was already inside them,
like it was already inside the Japanese,
like it was already inside just about everybody.

Long ago he fought down with fanatical tenacity

his fear of death in combat as he fought down
his learning disability as a boy
but his sickness at facing this uniquely
concentrated cruelty
he could not overcome.
So many times reading history
he emphatically
believed he had lived many ancient soldiers lives
so strong his empathy
but now he was the child led to this torture chamber
and he could not open the door.

"Send in the son-of-a-bitching krauts from the town to clean it up,"
he said to his aide after he turned and walked away.
"Make that bastard-Burgomaster and his wife go in first," he added.
Patton ordered so it was done.
The Burgomaster and his wife committed suicide soon after.

Man-Corn in the Promised Land III

A short history of man-corn in the USA. Looming insolvency of the local, state, and federal governments has made the casual cannibal jokes take on a more anxious tone...

It sounds like the beginning of another morbid joke:
Cannibal eats homeless man's face. Just like
the one about Jeffery Dahmer walks
into a bar, orders a beer with a little head on it.
No one sees the horror latent just below the surface,
waiting to emerge when things get bad.
The fattest people in the history of earth
including the poor obese poor,
moving in ambling herds
between the malls and sports stadiums
like self-satisfied woolly mammoths who cannot imagine
any real danger until they are chased off the cliff
with fire, straight into the cooking pits.

Right from the beginning,
in the winter in Jamestown 1609,
was the Starving Time. "One ravenous man fell upon
and ate his loving wife."
In high school history class the moving story of the stranded
Donner Party wagon-train from Springfield, Illinois,
the poignant funerals in the deep Sierra Nevada snow,
agreement that after singing
"We shall gather at the River"
the first to sneak back
at night could dig up the body.
The wise guy who sat behind me
interrupted class to recite a limerick he made up:
"Donner led

his friends out to find
new land freedom.
But instead he sat down to eat them."

Potatoes fried in melted Indian fat
from a burned down Creek Lodge;
Davy Crockett said he and his comrades
ate them until they nearly burst.
Mountain man Liver-Eating Johnson,
the real "Jeremiah Johnson,"
visualize buckskin-clad Robert Redford slicing open a Crow
Indian's gut and feasting on the raw liver in glorious Technicolor!

In 1878 after another too-late-in-the-year-to-cross-the-mountain-pass
screw-up
Alfred G Packer killed and ate: James Humphrey,
Frank "Reddy" Miller, George "California" Noon, Shannon Wilson Bell,
and Israel Swan.
The judge, a Democrat, spoke at the sentencing:
"When you came to Hinsdale County
there were seven democrats here. But you,
you man-eating son-of-a-bitch, you ate five of them!
I sentence you to be hanged by the neck until you're dead! dead! dead!"
But Packer the Republican cannibal went to a higher court
and had his sentence reduced
to forty years. He got out early for good behavior,
became a vegetarian.
1968 the students at the University of Colorado named their cafeteria
the "Alfred Packer Memorial Grill." They hung up a sign that read:
"Have a friend for lunch!"

General Patton Addresses the Poetry Conference

Reincarnated General George S. Patton, Jr. is called on to give a morale boosting talk at a conference of poets who are dealing with an outbreak of plagiarism on poetry posting websites.

"Attention!"
"At ease, sit down, lay down,
stand on your head if you want to.
Now I want you to remember
that no bastard ever
wrote a great poem by suffering for his art.
He wrote it by letting the other poor dumb bastard
suffer for his art
while the true poet lived life in a celebration of passion.
This English language the Bard-of-Avon
bequeathed to us four hundred years ago
has the best metaphors,
best alliteration, best imagery, and finest objective correlatives
in the world.

"You know, I almost pity the poetaster
and copy-write infringing bastards
we're going up against.
By God I do.
We're not just
going to figuratively shoot the plagiarist bastards;
we're going to symbolically cut out their living guts
and use them to grease the chains
on our bicycles before we peddle off to Starbucks
to get our morning lattes; we're going
to metaphorically murder those lousy Milli Vanillis

by the bushel.

"Now I know some of you guys and gals
wonder if you'll chicken out
when it comes time
to stand up and recite your poems
in front of other people. Don't worry
about it. I can assure you that when you get on stage
you will perform. If it's real it's in your blood.

"Truth and beauty are our objectives;
we are constantly advancing towards them.
Life lived authentically
is the strategy we use to achieve them.
Anything that cages human aspirations
for love and freedom
is the enemy.
Weigh into oppression with your verse;
shoot their pet dogmas in the belly!

"I don't want to hear about any holding
on to the past. Let the poetaster do that.
We are hanging on to only one thing
and that is the reader.
When he absorbs our stuff it's going to knock
him around until he doesn't know
what hit him and his life is changed forever.

"And you can forget about recreational
psychoactive
drugs,
Doors of Perception and all that. Once you've
tried to put your hand in the goo you think
your best friend's face has turned into

you'll know drug hallucinations are not inspiration.

"And there's another thing I want you to remember
and you can thank God for it.
Thirty years from now
at your fireside
with your granddaughter
on your knee
and she asks you,
'What did you ever do that was artistic?'
you won't have to say, 'Well, I
just phone voted for the least
shitty singer on "American Idol."'"

"Now you know how I feel. Go-on. I will be proud
to stand and deliver my poetry on stage with any one
of you wonderful guys and gals, at any poetry slam,
any time, any where.
That's all."

pOlItIcIaN

"If a society must have an ever-expanding list of laws to survive it doesn't deserve to." Chairman Wow

I'm not supposed to be loyal to you.
Look,
you're
a hired hand at best,
a gargantuan flesh-eating bacterium
in a suit and tie at worst.
I've watched you
kidnap the Constitution,
our precious Bill of Rights,
and like a skilled pimp
snatching a blond Moldavian
peasant girl
beat her down and then groom her with false
praise, rape her repeatedly
until she's perverted into some pliant,
omnivorous whore that just exists to make money
for you
and your unctuous cronies. The fiercest pirates
cruising the Arabian Sea hang their heads in shame
when comparing their piddly million dollar ransoms
to your extortion and squander of trillions and trillions!

The worst are you, you mild-mannered
shape-shifting, middle-of-the-road fascists
with your polling data and focus-group-approved
soundings. Constantly culling passionate debate
and passionate people so you can move the rest
of the heard into the slaughter pen without undo incivility.
After you've passed about ten million convoluted laws

that make everyone a potential felon you pick
which of them to enforce on who you want targeted,
squeezing that much closer to complete control.

When you're finally faced with your treason
you just spout standard condescending palliation,
standing stiffly between the armed guards in dark shades
and blue suits, about how no system is perfect,
it could be worse, be mature about this, don't criticize
the mainstream media even if they get caught spreading
lying propaganda because then you'll give
extremist media a foothold,
and at least you all ain't in some North Korean
concentration camp fist-fighting
for the undigested corn kernels picked out of the latrines.

False choice. You didn't make this country
we did.
We didn't make it with lobbyists and PAC money.
We made it with the most heroic word
in human language.

Potemkin Villages and Poetic Personae

Catherine the Great
in plush carriage rides
with her favorite Field Marshal,
Prince Grigory Potemkin,
on warm sunny days.
Farther and farther
into the Russian hinterland
each summer, touring villages
that are only perfect facades,
empty ghost towns built to fake
progress in the empress's realm.

Fernando Pessoa in Lisbon
writing at his translator's desk,
rejecting the Red riots
and the crowds at the fascist parades,
creates separate poetic personae.
His "Self," "The real Me,"
"My Soul," gives them names,
and explores the richness and depth
in those quite different but real personalities.

In our own time authenticity is absent all around us.
Integrity eludes. So many mocking the sincere artistic
efforts of others, snide glares at honest work,
sneers at faith and love of family. The future
they promise is another Potemkin Village.
Time to get alternate I.D.

A Plague of Lions

Glinting white mushrooms
sprouting out of the summer sky sapphire
become parachutes
with roaring cargo.

Beaming throughout the great land
a bureaucracy burlesque
of bulletins, bulwarks, and bullwhip cracking buffoons.

Blue metal barrels melting from nimiety,
still the leonine rain pours
ready-to-hunt prides.

Tawny maned fury mauling
our neighbor in his own back yard
as we look down from the attic window
like griffin vultures
waiting for our turn at the kill.

Knoxville Horror

Circle of piranhas
Mouths full
Of bullet-teeth
And blue pills
Orderly piranhas
Waiting their turns

Two young souls
Submerged
Under a river
Of burning bleach
Burning flesh
Mutilation
Gang rape
Media blackout

A nation
Half predator
Half prey
Cannot stand

Good Friday on the Rez

A pair of Ravens
One on the road
One on a pole

In Chicago
The children
Are slaughtering
Each other

Out on the rez
The children
Are made to run
After the Good Friday feast
To escape the demon Diabetes

Just south of the border
Right across the line
The children
Are being mowed down
Cartels like the hawks
That hunt in packs
Filling up mass graves
Quinceanera girls
All dressed up
With no place to go
But under the dirt forever

Somewhere out on the rez
They are making babies!
The kids like ripened fruit
Are falling from the trees
Plumb colored, roly-poly,

Hit-the-ground-running, kids!

In Connecticut
they are shooting down
The little Children
In China they are hacking
To pieces their little children

Outside the rez
Vultures are gathering
Better keep moving!

In Russia
The mothers
Forced to watch
Their children
Blown apart
With grenades

Meanwhile, out on the rez
The running little boys
Make silly faces
And the little girls laugh
Then the running little girls
Make silly faces too!

Way out on the rez
The elders pray
In the name
Of someone
Out loud in public ceremonies
No "Supreme Court" stops them!

Way, way out on the rez

The pair
Of ravens soars
High above
The hawks and vultures

Girl Trouble

Call me Asshole. A great beginning to a picaresque adventure, huh? Of course my real name is not A-Hole it's Bret Owens and I'm not chasing a great white whale. Truth is I'm on the run from anything female. Driving north on the Alaska Highway to a place called Yellowknife, Northwest Territories, Canada after cashing out from my last job in the Middle East, my most recent run-in with Girl Trouble.

Back up. Despite being raised by my grandparents, I had a normal life until graduating college. With my B.S. in public health from the Frontier University of Central Kentucky (that's right, F.U.C.K.) I was set to go out and stamp out disease and pestilence. Be one of the good guys. But my first mistake was marrying my college sweetheart right after graduation. Annabelle was a doll until we got hitched and then her hidden bi-polar disorder emerged suddenly when, after a long Saturday of me out inspecting special event food stands in Louisville, she decided I was really cheating on her and tried to stab me to death when I got home. Ruined my favorite leather jacket. The divorce was ugly, false accusations of abuse, etc.

After I healed up and the divorce was finished I had to get out of the state of Kentucky, shit, get out of the same hemisphere she was in. Landed a high-paying gig as a health inspector in one of the rich rich rich Gulf States. Everything went swimmingly for two years until I got a housefly complaint in one of the harems. So I go to this all-female complex, get escorted to this eighteen-year-old girl's private cottage.

Nasrine was half Arab half Swedish and was not in a veil. Fact is the girl was wearing next to nothing, cut-off tee shirt and short shorts. She turned down the screeching Scandinavian black metal music and then led me to her little kitchenette where there was one lonely housefly she demanded I dispatch with insecticide. I did and left, didn't think anything of it until the next day she called in another fly complaint. I go back out to that harem, no escort this time, walked by myself up to her cottage in the 120 degree blast furnace they call a normal day there, and she answers the door in a bikini.

Tried to play it cool but heck, I'm a healthy twenty-six-old dude who hasn't had any in two years, and anyway they always know when you think they have a great body. She led me back to the kitchenette and pointed to the dead fly in the window. I look at it close-up; it's definitely dead. The window sill like the rest of the place sparkling from the slave labor of a poor Filipino lady house cleaner; which means Nasrine saved the dead fly to get me back here.

I look up and she is there blocking the doorway out of the kitchenette. She had a smirk I'll never forget when she said, "Come to me and do what I say or I will report you."

So I was quasi-raped by an eighteen-year-old girl. Really shook me up, delicate cultural situation I was in and all. But the very next day she called the office and requested me specifically to come back out again. This went on for weeks, one time four days straight. Then silence, nothing, no contact. I thought this must be it; I was safe, she had found another victim. No chance! One Tuesday afternoon I was secreted a note that read: "ASSHOLE-AMERICAN! YOU GOT ME PREGNANT! YOU ARE DEAD MAN! ASSHOLE!"

Of course I panicked. Imagined her hiring some foreign laborer to off me for peanuts or her family finding out and doing it officially. That afternoon I bribed the red-bearded Scotsman M.D. at our ex-patriot health center to say I had a terminal case of prostate cancer. One fifth of contraband Jack Daniels was all it took. Then I purchased airline tickets and collected my pay. That night flying out of Dubai instead of feeling relieved I started playing out the scenarios for Nasrine. Probably she would just catch a flight somewhere and get an abortion. I doubted that her ultra-rich family would honor kill her if they found out; the males had pretty decadent reputations. She would certainly end up in whoredom though. Didn't really like the thought that now I'm just another bad guy looking after his own hide but that's the way it was.

After getting back to the States I got on a Greyhound bus, the most anonymous form of transportation, and headed west. Took about a week to figure out what I was going to do. When I finally came up with a plan I sneaked north across the border into Vancouver, British Columbia; tracked down a Chinese guy who sold me a high price, high quality fake Canadian identity. Only problem was the name: Francois Wong. I don't look like a Francois Wong.

Next I did some calling around at some far north public health agencies and landed a phone interview with a department director in Yellow Knife, Northwest Territories. It went well and he called back the next day telling me I had the job. The community was growing by leaps and bounds up there because of a new diamond mine. I converted the rest of my American cash and used it to buy a late model Toyota Land Cruiser and some expensive sub-arctic gear. I was broke but starting to sneak in a little survivor smile every now and then. Sometimes it's fun to be the asshole.

I turned off the Alaska Highway onto the Laird Highway. Thirteen hour drive ahead if a sudden snowstorm didn't hit. This newly paved road ran through some of the most serious wilderness left in the world. It was a partly cloudy but still cheery late August day and I was blasting out some old school Nirvana. Starting to transition from the sneaky asshole fun feeling of getting away with all my body parts intact to a flat-out everybody-can-kiss-my-ass euphoria.

The scenery was spectacular and there started to be a lot more wildlife. After the occasional browsing elk and bounding black-tailed deer in B.C., there now was serious-looking bull moose with their following herds of cows. Not long after spotting a few lone woodland bison near the road there were big herds blocking the road I had to stop and wait for. A black bear at one curve, a high-stepping herd of caribou around the next bend. No Ursus horribilis (grizzly) presented itself for viewing yet but they were out there. It was like traveling back to the Ice Age. Would have been no surprise to see a shaggy mastodon lumber out of the mysterious black spruce forest. Nope, no girl trouble out here!

I drove into the night but the aurora borealis was giving an incredible show so I drove off the road to park by a waterfall on the river to watch for a while. Through my small but powerful binoculars I studied the green and aqua and red veil undulating and shimmering across the far north night sky. Wolves started serenading and I decided to sleep here for a while. Just as I was dozing off the distant wolves stopped suddenly and then something else vocalized close by. Eerie, lonely wailing, long and drawn out, something with a diaphragm more powerful than anything I knew could be out here. I drifted off, but my sleep was tossing and turning. Incredibly I dreamed Nasrine was trying to warn me of some horrible danger.

When I woke up it was a foggy morning and I still had a bad feeling something wasn't right at this place. Stepped out to relieve myself and heard some weird grunting and whistling coming right out of the trees close by. That was it. I turned and jumped into the Land Cruiser and took off. Driving too fast and then some tall animal walking on two legs appeared out of the fog onto the road in front of me; I swerved to miss it and went over a hill and down into muskeg that stopped the SUV cold. Banged my head pretty good. I tried to get the vehicle rolling again but it was half sunk in the muck and wouldn't budge. Felt like I was going to pass out, there was a little blood dripping from my forehead so I crawled out with my thousand-dollar sleeping bag, a few flares, some emergency food bars, my weapon, and laid down not far from the road but not too close, hoping one of the truckers going past would see me. I managed to get inside the sleeping bag and blacked out.

When I woke up I was moving, fast. Still inside the bag bouncing up against a big, muscular body that was carrying me. A bad stench came off it that made me woozy and unable to do anything or even call out for help. Got drenched going across a large river. Twisted and turned through the forest until we reached a narrow box canyon that had lots of hot springs and even some geysers. My kidnapper climbed down a sheer canyon wall holding onto the sleeping bag with me in it like a sack of potatoes. I blacked out again.

I woke up on the ground. Sat up and looked around. Lovely little box canyon with a meandering creek and some beautiful aspens but too much like a pit. It was sunny now. A pebble hit my head and then another. Picked flowers covered me, blue crocuses and other flowers and even an orchid that I didn't think could grow in the far North. Turned around and there she was squatting fifteen feet away. Face more human than simian but not by much, covered with about an inch of dark auburn hair from pointed head to the broad feet, muscular arms and legs the same length, thick torso, and large black eyes that were looking off to the side coyly. She had pendulous hair-covered breasts, was definitely female. Something that could not and did not exist, according to everybody except the hundred or so people who claimed they saw one every year. A frigging Sasquatch.

She gave a sneering grimace with her mouth that I guess was supposed to be a smile, clacked her white teeth together and then stood up. At least seven and a half feet tall, seven hundred pounds. Then Queen Kong took two strides, bent down and picked me up, lifted me to eye level. Couldn't move, just kept repeating my alma mater's acronym over and over...

To be continued...

Girl Trouble (cont.)

I thought for sure Queen Kong was gonna bite my face off but instead pressed her forehead against mine for what seemed like minutes and then gently let me down. Felt there was buzzing inside my head, between my ears, couldn't think straight for a little while.

Q.K. left the pit, returning shortly with a gutted porcupine. My mind was clearing up. I noticed now there were lots of small animal bones scattered in front of a den. Mostly marmot and porcupine. She wasn't a vegetarian but the fact there was no big game and especially no human bones was a relief. She pulled the porcupine apart with expert dexterity, leaving all the quills on the ground, threw half of it not to me but to the grunting, hyperactive wolverine that emerged from the den. They seemed old friends; maybe even worked together as partners. The wolverine walked right up to me sniffing and then, like I was no big deal, went about his business.

Not knowing what else to do I sat down on a log and started munching on one of my power bars. How far was I from the highway? Dozens of miles certainly. Hundred miles from the closest settlement, the tiny village of Dene Indians called Nahanni Butte. I was in the middle of the Nahanni wilderness for sure. No one knew I was out here. No search party for a long time, maybe ever if the Toyota completely sank in the muskeg.

I looked Q.K. over again. Her intricate chattering sounded more emotive than informative to be a real language but it was close. What the hell was she? A leftover side branch of the Hominid family tree? Somebody experimenting with human genetics? Who knew. But then something like a movie popped into my head: I saw a large tribal group where all of the adults were killed off by hostile neighbors a thousand generations ago leaving little kids hiding in the forest to grow up without proper language or fire; each generation passing on more and more animalistic traits that helped them stay alive. A new species descended from us Homo sapiens.

After an hour or so of clearing my head and getting my strength back, I decided it was time to go. Sixteen hours of daylight this time of year up here but it was already half wasted I could tell by where the sun was at. Amazing how fast you can go from terror to shock to something close to Stockholm Syndrome to building rage. She was, after all, just another female trying to trap me, keep me from where I needed to be. I pulled out my .40 caliber Kimber pistol from my sleeping bag, cocked it, and cleared my throat.

"Look, darling, I know you know what this is. I know I don't have to make any ugly bang-bangs with it to impress you. We're all grown-ups here. I'll just put the whole thing down to you were just rescuing me from an accident, had no malicious kidnapping intent, got a little carried away and carried me away." I threw Q.K. my ball cap with the Arabic name of the public health agency I used to work for, should have gotten rid of it when I left the Mideast anyway. "Something to remember me by. Never met a girl like you before and I'll always remember you." Put my right hand over my heart and said, "Salam alikum." Thought that was a pretty classy kiss-off. Leisurely collected some flares and power bars, stuffed them in my parka but left her the expensive sleeping bag.

I went straight for the easiest rock wall to climb, put the pistol in my belt and started climbing. Used to do some rock climbing in school. Wasn't too worried about her coming after me. Her expression wasn't anger or fear when I pulled the gun it was more disappointment. Still I did a few quick glances back to make sure she was where I left her.

Made it to the top and started jogging downhill. Mackenzie Mountains all around, top half snow covered. White specks that were a mountain goat herd moving to my left; I headed straight down to what was certainly the Nahanni River. Might be able to get rescued from a party of late-season whitewater rafters. Rounded a bend around a copse of white spruce and there was the most gorgeous enticing girl I ever met in my life. Red wavy hair that fell about her shoulders, blue eyes that sparkled with intelligence, big smile that came from a generous soul who was not materialistic. Like someone read my mind and put together all the attributes that would make the ideal woman. She waved and I stopped in my tracks.

"Hi there," the girl said.

"Hi." I walked up to her and she slid her backpack off of her shoulders and put it on the ground.

"I'm Abigail," she said.

"I'm Bre..., I mean As..., I mean Francois."

"Francois?" Abigail said.

"Yeah, you can call me Frank. Hey, I don't want to come off like a nutcase out here but I'm trying to get away from a big animal I had a run-in with this morning."

"You had a run-in with an animal? What did it look like?" Abigail looked bemused.

"What it was isn't important. Seriously, we have to get out of here. You have a phone that works? A satellite phone or something? Mine got wet when I got dragged through a river. It couldn't get reception out here anyway. We need to call for a rescue, like right now."

"I don't carry a phone," Abigail said still bemused. "I have a two-way radio back at my cabin."

"Where's your cabin? Let's get going." I looked at her with my best serious, not-a-crazy-guy expression but she just smiled.

"It's ten miles away, down by the river." She nodded her head the general direction I was running when I first saw her.

"I'm telling you we're in danger standing here. We have to get moving!" I almost pulled out my pistol. Started looking around thinking Q.K. might change her mind and come after us. This girl Abigail was starting to tick me off.

"It must have been pretty scary to get dragged off by a Sasquatch," She said with a straight face.

"You know what happened to me?"

"I knew she snatched somebody this morning. I was tracking her carrying something about as heavy as a man."

"So you know they exist?"

"I'm a primate behavior doctorate from the University of Toronto," she stated. "I've been studying Sasquatch out here for two summers now. I know your girlfriend very well. She's a great big wild girl, the kind of girl who knows what she wants, but nice as long as you don't try to hurt her."

"How long has your university known they really exist?" I started walking towards the river. She picked up her backpack again and started walking beside me.

"A lot of people and governments have known they existed since the Patterson film," Abigail explained. "Hard for there to be legal protection for something that's not quite human. There's enough problem between different types of humans. But there is a bigger problem with letting the world at large know they exist." "What would that be?"

"They have special powers that could be militarily significant. They've evolved some unique abilities. Their nervous system, their brains evolved in a different direction than ours. There are a lot of powerful world players that want to get their hands on a live one. They have to be protected."

"Like who? What could a military do with a Sasquatch?"

"The Chinese military, the American defense industry corporations, the Russians, just to name a few. They want the secret of how Sasquatch changes the perception of reality in humans. Anyone that learns that ability will be able to defeat any enemy."

"Sasquatch can change the perception of reality in humans? That sounds like ESP bullshit. ESP is a pseudoscience. No one has a theory to explain it and no one can validate, reproduce studies that support it."

"Think about it. Human brains evolved to be good at behaviors other animals don't have, like ah..." Abigail couldn't come up with an example for some reason. Figured she was speaking a little awkwardly because she hadn't seen another human in a long time.

"Like math," I helped her out. "Controlling fire. Making complex tools."

"Right. Think about what a human brain is. It's a machine, like a car. Somebody has to drive it. You could say it is a machine built to be used by a ghost. Inside humans there is a conscious ghost and the subconscious ghost. When you sleep your subconscious ghost makes your mind build new realities. Most of the time when you're sleeping those realities seem as real as anything else. You can't tell the difference. Sasquatch has a nervous system that can project out their consciousness to operate a human brain. Under the right conditions they can make you think they are a tree stump, a boulder, another animal like a cougar. Think about how advantageous that would be to an animal competing with humans who use overwhelming technologies like guns and helicopters."

"It sounds interesting but a little too Jungian for me," I said. "I would have to experience it to believe it."

Abigail gave a sly smile. She spread her arms and turned in a freedom-loving spin with her eyes closed and her face in the sun then went back to normal walking again.

"So, do you have a guy back in Toronto or out here with you?" I asked because she was making me smile.

"No boyfriend. Field research is tough on relationships. How about you Frank? You hooked up with anyone?"

"Not currently," Looked back one more time to make sure Q.K. wasn't following. Was starting to feel less jumpy. "I have to say that your Sasquatch female friend, even after taking me home against my will, probably treated me better than the last two women in my life."

"So where were you heading to?" Abigail asked. Clouds were starting to roll down from the mountains.

"I was driving up from Dawson Creek B.C. trying to get to Yellowknife. Landed a new public heath job there."

"You could work here with me if you want," Abigail said out of the blue. "I could use a partner. You obviously have a connection with the primary female Sasquatch in this valley, can get way closer than she lets me get. We could really gain some valuable knowledge with you interacting with her."

"Working conditions are a little harsh out here. Aren't you afraid of the grizzlies?" Suddenly a silver gyrfalcon dove out of the sky and hit a ptarmigan that had been invisibly hidden in the bunch-grass just twenty feet in front of us. Abigail ignored it.

"Grizzlies don't come into this valley. The Sasquatch keep them out."

"You're not afraid of getting kidnapped by the Sasquatch then?"

"Only the dominant males are dangerous and they don't live around here most of the year. They travel far and wide, sometimes migrating way down into the States where they scare hillbillies in trailer parks." We both laughed and then she said, "There is one I call Skook who has a family group that passes through. When he does I clear out. Other than that it is pretty safe. So what do you say to my offer? You have a science background, this would be your chance to participate in some research that would make you famous when it finally is released to the public." She stopped, turned and looked me in the eyes.

"Right now staying anonymous is what my ambition is," I said but she was melting my resistance.

Abigail reached out and took my hand in her warm hand, "You can stay anonymous then. But I really could use you out here with me."

That about sealed the deal. I started moving in for the embrace but at that moment an echoing scream rose up so dreadful and piercing it nearly split the sky apart. Instead of jumping into my arms Abigail backed away, a look on her face I had never seen on anyone's face before.

"It's Skook," she said. "He's here."

(To be continued)

Girl Trouble (Finis)

"Abigail, I need to see what this Skook is; I have to see what I'm up against," I said but she didn't respond. "Take off then. Go back to your cabin." I turned and started out towards the screams that were really roars. Abigail reluctantly followed.

We hiked down a ravine and crossed a hot spring seep, climbed as stealthily as possible up to a ridge that looked down into a little valley. Got down on my belly and pulled out my small but powerful binoculars from my parka. There were six figures picking huckleberries down below. I studied the biggest figure, obviously Skook. Ugly, mean, nasty-looking brute. Over nine feet from the top of his smallish, pointy head to his over-sized hinged feet, greyish-white hair covering his whole body except the mostly hairless face gave him an eerie, hobgoblin look from a distance. He had no neck, was about eleven hundred pounds that packed in as much testosterone as two Super Bowl football teams put together. He uttered sinister, rapid-fire orders to the others that sounded kind of Japanese, a lot of rolling R's. Yeah, a giant hairy Samurai on meth. No way I wanted to go up against him even with a gun. He could have torn a silver-back gorilla apart.

Scanned over to the two next biggest figures, both were female. They looked kind of mangy and weatherworn compared to Skook or QK. One looked pregnant. Still, they were both way bigger than me and couldn't be disregarded. The next two figures were juveniles about five-and-a-half to six-feet-tall and they were both pug-ugly. Most baby mammals look cute but not those two. They ran around on all fours for some reason, I guess because their arms and legs were the same length. Made them look even creepier.

A small snowstorm hit just then, nothing serious, the kind of weather that passes through mountains in late summer. A tiny reminder of coming attractions. I thought this is good, will help keep them from picking up our scent. I wiped the snow from my hair and forehead then went back to studying them. Skook didn't pick any huckleberries; he visited each of the other troop members in turn, each one had to give up a handful or else

Skook thumped them a good one with the back of his ham-sized right hand. I guess Skook was a high-tax, big-government proponent.

"We have to get out of here now," Abigail whispered behind me. "It's a miracle Skook hasn't picked up our presence yet."

"Fuck him," I said. "They're all preoccupied picking berries now anyway." I finally put the binoculars onto the small last figure farthest from the others in the huckleberry patch. My mouth dropped open. I couldn't even cuss. It was a naked human girl, about ten or eleven. Her black Indian hair was long and disheveled, her face swollen from mosquito bites and scratches all over her arms and the rest of her body. Her mouth made the same kind of noises the others did and her eyes just looked like some kind of animal with a hint of sadness. The sadness of missing out being what she was supposed to be: a human being.

I back-crawled down the ridge then turned to Abigail. "You knew this troop of Sasquatch kidnapped a human child, didn't you?"

"What does it matter? There's nothing you can do about it anyway." Abigail kept nodding towards the ridge. "Skook is gonna kill us both."

"Look, Diane Fossey sacrificed her life trying to conserve the mountain gorillas she was studying in Africa but she would never have allowed them to snatch a human child. There is something bad wrong with you."

Abigail stood up and marched down the hill. I got up and followed her. Crossing the wet spot where the hot springs seep was I noticed some lynx tracks and my boot prints in the mud, next to mine Sasquatch tracks. No small, Italian hiking boot prints like Abigail was still leaving in the half inch of snow on the other side of the seep. Oh shit.

"Hey Abigail," I said, trying to act like I was an always-in-control, fearless bad-ass. "What's four times four?"

She stopped, turned slowly around and then walked back down to me. Looked like she was going to gently caress my chest but then I was knocked back about fifteen feet and got one mother of a quick flashing headache. When I could open my eyes again Abigail was standing over me but now Abigail had Queen Kong's face. The backpack on the ground transformed into my ball cap. She slowly turned and strode away, gradually the illusion she had put in my mind dissipated.

Queen Kong/Abigail turned and with one Sasquatch hand stuck her stubby middle finger up at me and then with her other hand showed me that she had my .40 caliber pistol. Looked small in her enormous hand. She strode away and disappeared into the trees. Flipped off and ripped off by a love-lorn Sasquatch. Almost got down and dirty with her too, when she disguised herself behind her Abigail illusion. Yuck.

I stood up and rubbed my temples. Now I had a decision to make. Take off and try to make it back then lead in a rescue party or go try to get the little human girl right now? Starting to think I was put here on purpose to make this choice. Was this upsurge of conscience a remnant of college humanism or of Sunday school? Maybe guilt over abandoning Nasrine? Remembered as a little kid how I snickered when the pastor taught the God of the Bible picks some unlikely characters to do important stuff, like Moses having a speech impediment and still had to lead the People Israel out of bondage. But how could somebody with my personality be a chosen hero? For whatever reason I decided I would have to do it, put aside my Asshole self, just on a temporary basis, to rescue that little girl.

I scooped up my baseball cap and ran crouching to a brushy, concealed spot downwind of Skook and his huckleberry picking troop of Sasquatch plus kidnapped human child. I duck-taped three .40 caliber bullets from my extra pistol clip to one of my road flares then lit it, left it on the ground, and ran crouching around the ridge again. The snow was down to flurries now and I had to move fast when I got upwind of them or they would catch my scent.

I ran until I got to the other end of the huckleberry patch then got on all fours and moved as fast as possible through the underbrush. The little girl was farthest from the others on this end of the berry patch. When the first round went off they all stopped and immediately stood upright facing where the bullet explosion came from, away from me, waiting for Skook to decide what to do.

The little human girl was about ten feet away when she noticed me and gave a weird warning cry. I jumped up and tackled her. She was scratching and trying to bite through my parka like a wildcat but I gave her one good punch on the chin and knocked her out. The other two bullets exploded and the Sasquatch scattered. I wrapped the girl in my emergency blanket, picked her up and ran, headed for the Nahanni River.

Threw her over my shoulder and tried to pace myself. If Skook vocalized I didn't hear it. Probably gave them a psychic message. If we get to the river I'll start a big fire. That should get somebody's attention. Hopefully keep these bastards back. Since they don't use fire they probably would be scared of it.

Followed an animal trail next to a growing stream that flowed fast down towards the river. Just when I thought we were maybe clear of them, one of the juveniles, a jet-black one, ran up out of the brush and nearly tackled us. I whipped out another flare, lit it, and had in right in his face.

"You don't like this, do you Junior?" I said. He disliked the smoke more than the flame, got up on two legs coughing, turned tail and ran. I threw the flare after him. Left me with a little buzz between my ears but that was about it. Walked for a while with the girl more comfortably in my arms. Trying to get my breath back then Skook stepped out from the some trees in front of us.

Supremely formidable, intimidating, overwhelming, like the whole Nahanni River valley come to life and striding up to swallow me up. I put the girl on the ground up against a boulder, turned and faced Skook with my last flare and my extra clip that had five or six rounds in it. Was going to burn off the bullets aiming at him as I held the clip. Didn't get to light the flare. I was down on my knees puking just from him looking at me. Seemed like he didn't want to touch me though. Maybe worried about catching something infectious from me?

The torture continued and grew more intricate, progressed from nausea to overwhelming dread. Then he put images in my mind of him tearing off my head or chewing on my genitals, really got old as he seemed to relish these two scenarios and made me go through them over and over. Just when I couldn't take it any more I remembered how Queen Kong reacted when I asked her the math problem, how it seemed to make her illusion dissipate.

Started asking him in my mind simple math problems then moved up to algebra. The projected nightmares into my mind ceased. He really didn't like math. Kept thinking about more complex equations from geometry and then calculus, which I despised myself but was now glad they made me take it.

Skook now looked like he was the one that was going to puke. But then he shook it off and came at me in two great strides, put one hand on my shoulder and one giant hand over my head, ready to decapitate me, but then something big flew in on top of him and got his grip off of me. I couldn't believe it! Queen Kong jumped him to save me!

I was knocked back to the boulder and couldn't do much but watch. Skook threw her down pretty quick but then QK's wolverine friend came out of the bushes and attacked Skook. Forget wussy grizzlies, wolverines are the bad-asses of the North. He chewed on the white Sasquatch's leg like it was a chew toy; Skook repeatedly kicked him away but the muscle-bound mustelid kept coming back for more. Queen Kong got up to make a run for it; then turned and threw something at me, which turned out to be my pistol. The female Sasquatch disappeared into the trees as I picked up my gun. The wolverine retreated now too and it was just me and Skook.

Got the gun off safety and started shooting at his feet; at this point I decided against wounding a big aggressive animal like him, just wanted to scare him.

Punk-ass Skook made himself invisible as he ran off, except he was too unsettled to keep his tracks from appearing in the half inch of melting snow. I shot twice more behind the tracks to keep him motivated to go in the right direction, which was away from me and into the brush. Now a Canadian military helicopter buzzed out of nowhere. Another mind trick? I waved and the chopper came back and hovered. I did a bunch of mental calculations but the helicopter stayed in the real. So me and the wild little girl were now rescued, sort of.

Three Canadian Special Forces soldiers jumped out of the helicopter pointing their assault rifles at me. No introductions, didn't say anything, with the chopper so loud couldn't have heard them anyway. I knelt down, put my pistol slowly on the ground then put my hands up. The kid was coming to and one of the soldiers got to her and injected her with a sedative. Seemed they knew she would be hostile. The other two finally got to me, patted me down then handcuffed my hands in front of me, picked me up and got me onto the chopper. Not gently I should add. I was being treated as an enemy.

No talking as the chopper gained altitude. The soldiers all business as they secured us and began giving first aid treatment to the drugged little girl. I sat cross-legged on the floor, looked out as we were about to clear the highest ridge. Out of nowhere Queen Kong jumped onto the helicopter, hung onto a skid. The Special Forces guys and the pilot were immediately overwhelmed by whatever illusion she was putting into their minds. They dropped their weapons and clawed at their own faces. The pilot lost it and we started spinning in circles, going down pretty fast.

"Look, this obsession on me is poison for both of us," I spoke to her with my mind. "You have to get a realistic attitude about relationships. Forget the alpha males like Skook or the mysterious tall dark strangers like me. Those kinds of dudes just wind up hurting you. You're just like a lot of girls I've known. You're sensitive and you're smart, but for some reason you keep making bad decisions about guys. Give yourself a break! Find a kind of shy Sasquatch guy that you can invest in, if you know what I mean. You help build up his confidence and he'll be grateful and give back the emotional support you're craving." The chopper was just about to crash. "I want you to be happy," I said with my mind real quick.

QK gave the saddest but accepting look I ever saw and then let go of the helicopter skid. I didn't see where she landed but I know we were close to the ground. The pilot got it together and stopped the chopper from falling, stabilized it, and then got us out of the valley. The Special Forces guys slowly recovered and then acted like nothing had happened.

"So tell us again, Wong, what were you doing in the western part of Nahanni Park?" The Captain asked for the tenth time. I was in an orange prisoner's jumpsuit in the security interrogation room in the Yellowknife Airport, my hands still handcuffed in front of me. The five Special Forces guys glared at me across the table. The biggest, a corporal, let off some inappropriate laughter at hearing my new last name of "Wong."

"For the tenth time, I didn't know what part of the park I was in. Had no way of knowing. Something dragged me there after I had a wreck on the Laird Highway." I decided to play dumb. Was always my first choice when confronted by authorities with guns.

"No way something dragged you seventy kilometers through that terrain in a couple of hours. You had a handgun. You were in an area that's off-limits, quarantined, not even First Nations or biologists go in there. Bush pilots aren't allowed to even fly over the area." He paused before hitting me, finally, with what he wanted to know. "Are you a merc, yank? Did an American corporation or the Chinese or somebody else send you in there? What were you looking for?"

"I'm no Yankee," I stated very convincingly. "I'm Canadian. Was adopted by a French-speaking Chinese couple from Montreal. Grew up in Vancouver. You have my I.D. The permit for my pistol is in my billfold. I'm no mercenary; there's a public health job waiting for me here in Yellowknife. Check it all out if you don't believe me."

"You talk like an dipshit from West Virginia," the corporal said. He kind of looked like a downsized version of Skook.

"Never been there," I said. The corporal was really irritating me with his sloppy bad-cop routine.

"You have serious knife-wound scars on your chest," the Captain shifted gears. "You ever in the service? Ever in the 'Stan? Seems like you know how to handle yourself."

"Never was in any military," I said. "Was over in the U.A.E. for a few years as a civilian contractor, non-security work. Been in some tight places, learned how to deal with it. I don't take orders very well so I never considered joining any military." The Captain really didn't like what I just said about not liking to take orders. Must have been a sore point.

"So was it a female Sasquatch or a male that dragged you off to be a love-slave?" the corporal asked. "How was it?"

"It was a big hairy hermaphrodite, just like your mom." I replied and glared back at the corporal. Had decided to try to provoke them into roughing me up so I could go for a lawsuit, get something on them.

"You got a real mouth on you," the corporal said, eyeballing me intensely.

"You know...someday it might even get me into trouble," I said. He tried to cuff me but I got my hands up and stopped the minor blow. There was a scuffle that was not very graceful and it took a minute or so to get me back in my seat. Unfortunately no bumps or bruises.

"Look, I just want the truth, Bret Owens. Yeah, we know your real name. What were you doing in the Valley of Headless Men in Nahanni, a place nobody comes back from? How did you get that little girl away from them? Why did you have a handgun?" The Captain suddenly looked ripe for a deal.

"I'll talk just to you," I offered. "No hired hands need to know my business. No recordings."

The Captain stood me up then led me out by the arm into the hallway. It was just him and me. I looked carefully around then started talking. He took it all in, only asked me to repeat a few things.

"So you had the handgun because you were worried about your girl-friend's male family members?"

"That's right. I committed a big insult to a family's honor over there. The family is pretty important in the royal hierarchy; they wouldn't let it slide no matter how decadent they are. I have to carry protection." He looked satisfied with what I said.

"How did you get that little girl away from the Sasquatch?" The Captain seemed impressed.

"I used a diversion with a lit flare to set off some extra bullets. It was a lucky turn of numbers on the roulette wheel, I guess." I was happy how low key I kept the explanation. "So are you going to get the little girl back to her family?"

"No, she's going to a secret military base in the States for quarantine. Close contact with an unknown primate is serious business. Novel viruses and who knows what else she's been exposed to. They'll take good care of her but she'll never see the light of day again."

"Sounds like they have other cases there, other wild kids," I said but he didn't answer.

"I'm letting you go," the Captain said. "I don't have to tell you that if you open your mouth to anyone about this, try to sell your story, you'll end up where no one will ever find you."

I nodded my head affirmatively. They gave me back my stuff, minus my .40 caliber pistol. As he escorted me to the door that led out of Airport Security he stopped me to say one more thing.

"The reason we found you is that you had a tracking device in your baseball cap. Someone from Chicago, a young lady named Stephanie Pergroski, was in a panic to find you. Just thought you should know. Good luck to you, Mr. Wong."

Of course when I walked out into the airport terminal there was Nasrine bundled up like it was the middle of winter, waiting for me.

I walked with Nasrine up to the life-sized sculpture of the polar bear hunting a seal. There were a lot of people coming and going for a small airport terminal.

"You here to make me a dead man?" I asked her. Suddenly felt really tired. No more running.

"I am sorry I threatened you," she said. Sounded like a completely different girl. "I am not a bad person. My father and half-brothers were making me crazy. They wouldn't let me go live with my mother in Stockholm, wouldn't let me go to a university. They wanted me to marry an old cousin. The man is fifty-three! If I didn't they were going to put me in a whore-house."

"So what do you want to do?" I had to fight back an urge to hug her.

"I want to be with you. I swear I will give you no trouble. When you come home from work I will bring you tea." She was giving me the doe-eyes. Had to admit it was working.

"What about your family?"

"I ran away when we went shopping in Dubai. No one knows I'm here. I bought a false identification. I have an American passport now. My new name is Stephanie."

"You saved my life, Nasrine; I am much obliged. Clever girl, putting a tracking device in my hat." I smiled and then she did and we both started laughing. "So do you want to be a mom?"

Nasrine nodded yes and I did hug her, then gave her the End-of-World-War II-Sailor kiss. Delighted the Passersby. You can guess the rest. Not exactly happily ever after but close enough.

On these long, northern Canada winter nights when it's my turn to walk my new daughter to sleep, I wonder about the Sasquatch. What if there were a few that could weave intricate illusions? What if they came in out of the wilderness and learned to fool the masses, make themselves popular without any achievements or real talent. I'm not saying the Kardashians or W. or O. or Joe B. or Sarah P. is really a Sasquatch, but I'm not saying they're not...

Finis?

Man-Corn in the Promised Land IV

33 AD--Five bearded men discuss a recent public execution while standing in a circle alongside a busy, dusty road outside of Jerusalem in the Roman Judea province.

"Salvation from eating another man's flesh? Drinking his blood?" The first man said. "That man was insane! Insane, I say!"

"It was symbolic," The second man responded. "He taught in parables. The man was a holy prophet of peace."

"Ha! He was no prophet. What kind of holy prophet associates with women? One was even a prostitute!" The third man spat on the ground.

"He said he came to bring the sword, not peace," the fourth man put in.

"That's right, he was a bully!" The first man almost shouted. "He beat the money changers, with a rope, chased them right out of the Temple grounds. He even intimidated the Temple guards. They did nothing to stop him."

"He was a drunkard," the third man said. "His disciples were swindlers and rogues. The two big fishermen are well-known barroom brawlers. They call them the 'Sons of Thunder.' Another of those disciples is a Zealot, one of those bitter, anti-government extremists who cling to their swords and their crazy end-of-the-world religion. What he led was more like an outlaw gang than anything else."

"What do you say about the man they crucified?" the second man, the youngest, asked the fifth man, who had been silent during all this.

"What he said about eating his flesh and drinking his blood was meant to shock you," the tall fifth man said. He looked shrewd, like a man used to working with his hands and his head. "He meant it literally, in that you must eat his flesh with an earnestness you never had to eat anything before. It is the only way you can be made to face the crisis of corruption that is all around you. Propriety, living in conformity by eating correct food, having correct rituals or correct politics, like the Pharisees, blinds you and puts you on the road to Hell."

"How could that be true?" The first man clawed at his wavy hair. He looked like he wanted to tear out the image he had of himself as a ghoul raiding a cemetery to eat another man's flesh. "Cannibalism and Anarchy to reach salvation? Everything of value caste into the gutter to gain his salvation?"

"If the lion eats the man, the lion is blessed with life," the fifth man responded. "If the man eats the lion then the man is blessed with life. Despite this blessing, either the man or the lion will soon become hungry again. But if the man eats the flesh and drinks the blood of the Son of Man, the Lion of Judea, then he will be blessed with eternal life and never really go hungry again."

"There goes two of his disciples now," the fourth man said after they had all been silent for what seemed a long time.

"What is your name?" the first man meekly demanded. "Who are you?"

"You know who I am. I have no more time for talk." The fifth man started off to catch up with the two disciples.

The Bird Who Sings with Her Wings

The seine that nets out
the life you need to live
must not be allowed to rot
so I spread it out to dry.
The sleek, crow-sized bird
flew into my net as I slept.
A mysterious feathered
creature: sensitive gaze
in her knowing sepia eyes,
strong beak, scarlet crest,
ivory streaks along her black
neck and face. Music singing
from her wings when she flew.

I wanted to immediately release her.
But to set free the mysterious bird
without permission was impossible.
"It is a new species!" the authorities
barked (like small dogs in trailer parks).
"What if it is a bird that pecks out the eyes
of lambs or infants?" "What if it is beauty
in disguise?" Such a dangerous corporeality
cannot be allowed to fly free
in this overcrowded country
that survives only under the strictest discipline.

Wherever I went the answer was the same:
"We don't want that new bird soaring
over our back yards." Surprisingly captivity
with me seemed to suit her even though
I know nothing about the proper care

for such an avian. I only know she
likes to nestle inside my shirt, next
to my beating heart. Sometimes unnatural
habitats are ideal.

Eternal Universe?

If this universe were eternal
you would be reborn.
Approaching but never arriving infinity
would sooner or later randomly bring
your scattered atoms
back together to remake your exact body.

More than that: eventually
one of your multiple rebirths
would happen in exactly
the right circumstances
so that the same life experiences
would give you the same personality
you now have.

Some day a re-birth
giving you your body and persona
back would happen at a time
when death is banished by technology,
made illegal by some cosmic super-state
bureaucracy, and you will seek death but not find it.

Even more than that: ultimately
the high-tech cosmic super-state will latch
all your memories of past lives
onto you until your mind is overwhelmed with eons; your soul
a game piece, a library entry, or currency, or some other resource
to be used and abused by those with ultra-intellects.

But this universe is not eternal.
It was born painfully and grew gloriously
with risings of stars, nebula, and creatures.

End, built in, the entropy built in,
life span death sentence like in our DNA.
And with its demise my Christian anarchist heart
soars as high as the geese flocking over the Himalayas.

Old Book at the Crying Tree

--1912--

It was awful
but it was real,
Doctor George Zeller wrote:
I saw it,
one hundred nurses saw it
and three hundred spectators saw it...

He had gone mad
at the printing house
where he worked, they said,
when they brought
the sturdy but mute man
from the Chicago poorhouse
to the Peoria State Hospital.
A. Bookbinder was now his name.
He soon came to be known as Old Book.

Doctor Zeller, the new superintendent,
a reformer, removed
the words "Incurable Insane"
from the name
of the asylum, removed the bars
from the windows, and the restraints
from the patients.
Gave Old Book
the job of digging the graves
for the deceased.

At each funeral,
after the choir,

Old Book leaned
against a great elm tree,
in the middle of the cemetery,
removed his cap and wept
vociferously for the dead man
whether he knew him or not.

The years passed.
One day Old Book died.
After the choir sang
"Rock of Ages" the four
pallbearers heaved up the ropes
under the casket and fell flat
on their backs.
A baleful wail rose up.
When the hundreds
of mourners in broad daylight
turned to see
Old Book was there
at the Crying Tree.

Panic ensued.
Doctor Zeller ordered
the coffin be opened.
As soon as they did
the keening apparition
vanished.
Old Book lay inside
and the man's weight
returned to the casket.

Soon after the great old tree
died from disease.
Doctor Zeller ordered

the Crying Tree
cut down. But when they tried
a grim moan rose up
with each chop until the workmen
could not stand it and ceased.
Later they tried to burn the dead tree
but an even worse wailing erupted
so Doctor Zeller ordered that they leave
Old Book's Crying Tree alone.

Future-Snake

One November on a cool afternoon
in the Arizona desert foothills
I saw the biggest rattlesnake.
A lengthy western diamondback
coiled tight over a rodent burrow.

I threw pebbles to make
him slither.
Forked tongue eased out
then he knew what I was.

Sluggish he moved,
as if to say "You son-of-a-bitch,"
unwound down into the hole.
When only black rings and rattle were visible
there came a vision:
---------------------Snow covered mountainside
---------------------Twilight outside a village
---------------------Of ragged pygmies cowering in tunnels
---------------------Camouflaged dragon-ferret without legs or ears
---------------------Nightmare sixty feet long
---------------------Bright amber eyes
---------------------Covered in soft mottled down
---------------------Complex tail organ that could sound like:
---a baby crying
---a woman in distress
---seductive music

---------------------Undulating in and out of the snow
---------------------Around the pines and into a grotto
---------------------Warm-blooded cunning killer supreme
---------------------Hunting the scattered descendents of humanity.

Crazy Haiku

My skull cracks open
Painfully, wet and gooey
A condor emerges

Paradox #1

Real life
is
based on
a true
story.

Riddle #1

If spiders
were given
beautiful wings
would they
become butterflies?

The Mysterious Castaway

Based on a Legend from Maritime Canada.

1863 Nova Scotia

It was a misty summer noon.
The children playing on shore
watched with gaping mouths
as a sleek metallic vessel, lines
unlike any ship the progeny
of experienced
seafarers had seen, cruised
into Sandy Cove and deposited
a man into the water. The gleaming
ship sped off into the haze and was never
seen again.

They rescued a man a few minutes later.
A fine figure of a man, regal face
with a Mediterranean complexion
but light blond hair. Both his legs
had been amputated above the knees,
cauterized expertly, the doctor admitted.

When the young man came to
he spoke
in a language no one understood.
The doctor later made notes
on the syllables and his peculiar uniform.
Once he was made aware of where
he was the mysterious young man
never spoke willingly to any adult.
They decided to call him Jerome.

For a few years the Acadian villagers
tried in vain to get Jerome
to speak. He voiced only to children
or when surprised by a stern query,
and then would give an angry reply
in gruff but dulcet tones.

They brought in expert linguists from America
but the witnessed snatches of words that Jerome
used were related to no known language.
He spent most of the rest of his life in a wheelchair
doing one of two things:
watching the distant ocean vista
in all weather conditions,
sometimes speaking to children
in his mellifluous tones when no adults were present;
or when the weather was too bad
for months at a time he sat before a mirror
like a man watching himself
being tortured by life's natural
aging process. Eventually Jerome
was put in a pay-to-see exhibit,
fierce rage in his eyes, like
a man who awakes to find
he is displayed in a zoo run by baboons.
He died in 1912, an enigma never reveled.

Should Have Been a Nightmare

The sky had all the vibrant colors
and textures of javelina road kill.
Should have been a far future nightmare,
about half a billion years ahead,
I'd say. On the rocky, barren landscape
that had long forgotten human beings,
a German shepherd-sized scorpion
emerged from a trap door burrow.
So much detail, I could tell evolution
finally gifted our arachnid friends
with a closed circulatory system
so now they could get big.

It did not speak but I knew
by its intricately clicking mandibles
that the brain contained sentience,
its pinchers able to do complex tasks
but I could not imagine what.
It froze to stare at me, an astro-projected
specter to it no doubt, and heart-breaking
terror overcame it. The eight legs scrambled
for its trap door, sliding sideways in the dust,
crashing into a boulder, finally escaping down
into the safety of home.

Amazed, I woke up feeling happy and powerful.

The Face From the River

July 1918. Excursion steamship Columbia on the Illinois River. Five hundred passengers. Disaster hits.

Steamboat capsizes
Eighty bloated bodies beach
Near Peoria

Searchlights scan the fog
Upriver the coroner
Records notes on teeth

Now under black earth
Once under the dark brown flood
They found all but one

Stench of rotting flesh
Bleached ghost white from sun
Floating ever down

Netted his corpse while
Seining for gizzard shad, face
Covered...crawdads...

The Importance of Forgetting

In the secret corporate
biotech laboratory,
two white-coated men
watch the sixteenth mouse
tremble with fear, immobile
after one mild electrical shock
that would not have fazed
a normal mouse.

The subject
another prime
specimen from a new,
multimillion dollar,
genetically-engineered,
super intelligent, memory
enhanced, lab-mouse
bloodline
that solves problems,
learns mazes faster,
remembers cues
like no other rodents
in history.

After the mouse
dies in a final paroxysm
of shaking terror,
the senior PhD
says to the junior PhD,
"Well, I guess it's
important to be able
to forget."

Sex Zombies Must Die! Part 1

"Your little brother Robby is getting some pussy," Stacy Masters announced when she came in through the front door. The short, twenty-six-year-old blonde was stronger than she looked. She walked through the dining room and into the kitchen lugging a case of Mexican beer for their usual Friday night poker game.

"How do you know?" Ray Llewellyn looked up from divvying out the poker chips at the big round table. Clarence Carter and Tony Thomas sitting on either side of Ray both snickered.

"I heard serious love hollering when I drove up there to see if he was coming over tonight. That's why he wouldn't answer the phone." She was speaking from the kitchen, clanging out bottles from the case to put into the refrigerator.

"So he was being noisy?" Tony asked. His leering grin forced his shaggy dark brown eyebrows up into what Stacy always thought looked like devil horns.

"No, she was." Stacy came in the dining room and gave each of the three guys an opened bottle with a sliced lime. "Girl has a pair of healthy lungs. It was operatic. I could hear her all the way down the block."

"Who's his new girlfriend?" Clarence asked. "Is it that red-head girl he met from..."

"Never mind all that," Ray's grey eyes stared way too seriously up at her. "What do mean you could hear her down the block? That house is right next to the graveyards."

Stacy stood there in her tight "Gun Ho Doc!" good luck tee shirt her commanding officer had given her when she left Afghanistan. That had been her nickname over there for thirteen hellhole months. She studied her boyfriend Ray's face for a second then took a long swig from her own long neck bottle. "Yeah, sooooo?" she finally asked. It had always been easy to be friends with guys but hard for her to start a romance. Of the three previous serious relationships she'd had so far two had ended when the guy had started acting up in lunatic ways she couldn't figure out. Now this from Ray, a guy she'd been with longer than anyone else and who she really cared about, to the point she had just about decided he was the one. Please don't say anything deranged, she thought.

"Get the guns out of the safe," Ray ordered. "We've got to get up there right now. I'll tell you why on the way."

"Damn, when you said get the guns, Ray, that made me nervous, man." Clarence looked confused in the back seat of the SUV as they drove up the darkly lit road.

Ray for all his hurry was driving very slowly. He slowed down even more when they passed some guy walking unsteadily on the sidewalk of the oak tree lined residential street. Ray looked the pedestrian over with a strange, pensive look on his usually fun-loving face. Stacy saw he judged the guy walking was a normal drunk and he sped up again. She was putting her blond hair up into a ponytail while keeping the H&K assault rifle barrel upright between her legs. This was just nuts. Only Tony looked unfazed, a cigar hanging out of his mouth. She pointed into the review mirror. "Don't you light that thing in my car, asshole."

"Okay, okay," Tony said and chuckled. He loved to yank her chain.

"This is what's going on," Ray started. "When I graduated from college five years ago I was recruited by the C.I.A. My job was in a top-secret lab on the other side of the graveyards, up the bluff between the golf course and the Emergency Management bunker for the county. All I really did was take care of the rhesus monkeys they used in the experiments.

"The second month I was there, these black ops guys brought in this weird chemical they said they got from the Israelis, who said they somehow stole it from the Iranians who got it from the North Koreans. They said the chemical was used by the North Koreans for torture, to keep the tortured person from passing out when the pain got to be too much."

"Obama banned torture years ago," Stacy said. "If we don't use torture anymore why would they want to experiment with stuff like that?"

"Of course Obama banned torture," Ray said with a faint smile. "The way they justified working with it was claiming we are only developing counter measures to it, just like we keep manufacturing nerve gas supposedly only to find ways to deal with that. Anyway, the C.I.A. chemists working up there improved it, made it so the nervous system of those monkeys wouldn't stop functioning even if all their other organs were dead. Heart stopped, no blood circulation, kidneys stopped, liver stopped, lungs stopped breathing, everything stopped; the fucking monkey would still be screaming and jumping around inside the cage like they'd gone insane. That's why I quit. I couldn't take that animal abuse they were doing."

"Dang, that's raw," Tony said. "That's fucking raw!"

"So what's that got to do with your brother having some good sex at his house by the graveyard?" Stacy asked. This story was nuts. She knew he had worked for the federal government before they met but this was just whacked.

"They let the containers leak. Gallons and gallons of that crazy chemical went down into the dried up creek bed that runs through the middle of the graveyard. That bad spring flood last year turned the cemetery into a swamp for a month. All of the corpses buried in cheep, flimsy caskets would have been contaminated then. If something is dead already and then gets contaminated with that shit they will get reanimated if they get the right audio stimulus."

"What kind of 'audio stimulus' would 're-animate' them?" Stacy was just trying to humor him. How could she have not known she was living with a paranoid-delusional guy for a year and a half?

"What did you hear coming out so loudly from Robby's open bedroom window when you drove up to his house tonight?" Ray slowed down to look over another pedestrian. They were almost there. Robby's small, one story house was at the end of the block, the last one before the graveyards.

"Oh, give me a fucking break, Ray." Stacy said. "Her loud moaning is going to wake up the dead?"

"What are they gonna do when they come back, Ray?" Clarence almost sounded gleeful. He loved horror movies. "They gonna come out and start eating people?"

"No, not eat people." Ray steered the SUV into the driveway of his brother's house. He craned his neck out the driver's side window to stare into the darkness uphill in the woods at the border of the graveyard. "What they are going to do are rape people. Rape anybody they catch to death."

Sex Zombies Must Die! Part 2

"Remember, if the government finds out I told you three about this top secret torture chemical turning lab animals into sex crazed zombies, it's life in prison for me." Ray got out of the SUV followed by Stacy with the assault rifle. Clarence and Tony got out and Ray had Stacy give a 9mm pistol to Tony and a short pump shotgun to Clarence. Ray led them up the walkway to the small house.

"There's no bullets in it yet, but don't point it at anyone, shithead," Stacy said to Tony.

"Dang, no respect," Tony said, as he held the pistol sideways, posing like a goofy gangster in a cheap exploitation movie. From the dark, humid night far up the hill in the cemetery, only Tony caught the faint, faraway sound of wailing. It shut him up.

"Why give me the shotgun?" Clarence complained as they waited for Robby to answer the door. "You just think I can't shoot straight enough to handle a pistol."

"I just don't think an accountant that's never shot a gun before can handle a pistol." Ray said as he lightly rapped on the front door again. "Shotguns are easy, point and shoot. Takes a few shots to get used to the kick."

"Watch you talkn' 'bout." Clarence pushed his nerdy glasses up the bridge of his nose with a chestnut brown hand. "We C.P.A.s are O.G." Ray almost laughed.

Robby, shirtless, finally opened the door. He was a couple of inches taller than Ray. He put his hands up when he saw all of them openly carrying guns. Ray led everyone inside as Robby backed up towards his bedroom door.

"Listen, I'm sorry I didn't make it to the poker game tonight, but don't you think this is a little bit of an over-reaction?" Robby looked half joking and half serious. Just then a lovely young girl stepped out of the bedroom behind Robby. Her red hair was disheveled and she looked like she had gotten dressed in a hurry. Robby finally put his arms down and introduced her as Samone who happened to be the lead singer of an all redhead girl band called Amber Orgasm. Robby's band had played on stage with them at the last open air concert in the park.

"I've heard... so much about you." Stacy side glanced at Tony as she shook hands with Samone. This caused Tony to guffaw in his irritating, self-indulgent way.

Tony finished snickering and then lined up with Clarence to get Samone's autograph. Over his shoulder Tony partially overheard Ray talking in a low voice with Robby about the situation. Apparently Robby knew about the zombie monkeys Ray used to work with. Realization hitting that this was for real. Dang, Tony thought, I need some weed to deal with this. Or maybe some whiskey. Creepy that sound coming from up the hill.

"So you guys saw our show last Saturday night?" Samone asked.

"No," Clarence answered. "But we've heard all about your awesome vocal work."

"Thanks, I guess," Samone looked around very aware that these people were all acting weird. "What's with the guns?"

"Listen, Samone, you stay here and keep the door locked. If someone other than one of us starts banging on the door don't open it no matter what, okay?" The girl looked wide-eyed but shook her head in the affirmative. Ray then looked around at the others. "We have to move fast. Hopefully there won't be too many of them."

As soon as they stepped outside a series of wails greeted them from up the hill. Tony came out last.

"This is some shit; this is some shit," he kept saying out loud to himself. He watched Robby slip into the garage and come out with a sledgehammer.

"Do we go for the head, smash their brains?" Clarence asked.

"No, aim for the genitals," Ray said. "A good crushing blow down below should do it. We don't have big enough weapons to do enough damage to their skulls. For some reason a shocking hit down in the privates worked on the zombie monkeys. The only way a live monkey stopped a zombie monkey was by biting hard on the zombie's genitals."

"There you go Tony; if you get into a tight place just bite their balls!"

"You can bite me, Stacy!" Tony responded.

At Stacy and Tony's exchange, tension relieving laughter broke out between everyone but Ray. He hushed them as the wailing and now groaning moved closer.

Ray led them up a minibike path. Before they got to the first row of tipped over headstones they saw the emaciated figure silhouetted against the half moon lit night sky. "The rules of engagement are that Robby will try first to take them out with the sledge hammer. He has the longest reach. If there get to be too many I will shoot them one shot at a time. If there are too many for me then Stacy will go after them with the HK rifle. If we get like a hundred I'll have Stacy give you guys ammo. It's one week until Fourth of July; maybe the cops will think it's just kids setting off fireworks or if they do believe it's real gunfire then they probably will be too chicken to come up here without a lot of backup which will take hours. Any questions?"

"Ray, if this is for real why not get the Feds in here to take care of their own problem?" Stacy asked.

"The Company(CIA) contingency plan is to make it our problem," Ray said, anger dripping from his voice. "The government is going to quarantine the city and let everyone get killed. That's their plan, to blame it on a new chemical formulation for a meth-type drug. Their black opts agents will set up a phony drug lab up here in the graveyards and blame us semi-rural fly-over people for the carnage. Think of all the families with little kids in our neighborhood, Stacy. They don't deserve to be raped to death and then have a corrupt government blame the victims."

They walked up to the first figure that was awkwardly making its way down the cemetery hill towards them. At least a dozen other moving silhouettes were visible now starting about a hundred feet behind the first one. About twenty feet in front of it, Ray shined his hunting flashlight in its face, beam with a red filter to keep the light inconspicuous. It was a short, wrinkled faced man dressed in an old fashioned suit, probably buried in the 1950s. His face was discolored to a dark mildew blue coloring Ray had never seen before. Desiccated and slowly shuffling with his pants dragging, still around the ankle of his left leg, sunken eyes that probably couldn't see anything anymore.

"How can that thing have an erection when its heart isn't working?" Stacy asked.

"Men die with erections all the time," Ray responded. "You never saw that episode of the cable TV show about the family of morticians? Smoothing out corpse erections is one of the first things they learn." Ray could tell she believed him now. She hadn't though until right this instant. "Okay, Robby."

Robby walked up with the sledgehammer and swung it but the blow was an inch too high and the thing doubled over forward onto the hillside with a gigantic dry weez. Suddenly Stacy ran over to the zombie, bent down grabbing it by its wrists like her Navy corpsman training had taught her to do with a wounded hostile combatant.

"Stacy, don't touch it!" Ray yelled.

"I have to know this is really happening, Ray," she said and then stood up. "Destroy it, Robby, it doesn't have a pulse."

Robby stood close in front of the writhing thing and brought the sledge hammer down hard between its legs. The smack sounded wet and it let off a quick grunt and then a slow expiration of air. Old embalming fluid smell filled the air.

"Man, why don't they shut up!" Tony said and covered his ears. In front of them up the crest of the hill dozens more had appeared and they were all wildly wailing in unison, the closest ones grunting and groaning. Most were moving faster than the one Robby just took out.

"They are waking themselves up," Ray said. It had probably been just a few very close graves that the girl Samone had awakened. If only we had gotten up here sooner. He could tell Tony was about ready to loose it. Guys with the biggest mouths are almost always the most insecure, his father had told him a long time ago. "Let's get them." But after just fifteen minutes of hammering down two of the faster pantless rape-ghouls, all four of the zombie slayers were running down the path towards Robby's house with Tony in the lead.

Sex Zombies Must Die! Part 3

"What are we gonna do; what are we gonna do?" Stacy spoke loudly over the din of dead arms banging against the front door of Robby's house. They were under attack by at least twenty living-dead, sex-fiend ghouls, outside on the front porch of the small house.

"We'll go out Robby's back bedroom window, get in his pick-up and lead them back up into the cemetery," Ray said. "We need some way to get their undivided attention. We can't let any of them wonder down the street into the neighborhood."

"How are we going to get their attention, Mr. Zombie Expert?" Stacy cocked the HK assault rifle, readying to unleash bullets through the front door. Now there was wild moaning along with the banging on the door and it was overwhelming. Tony stood in the corner of the living room hyperventilating. Robby and Clarence pushed back against the front door but it was just a few seconds away from caving in.

"You and Samone get in the back of Robby's truck, stand up and make out with each other while we drive up the minibike path."

"What?" Stacy's mouth dropped open. "Are you serious?"

"You heard me Stacy!"

"Listen, I'm not gay; I'm not bi. Just because I fought with marines and shot at scumbag Taliban in Afghanistan...Anyway why not have Clarence and Tony make out. That homoerotic color coordination is big now."

"I know you're not a lesbian. You two have to do it, Stacy. Only a very small percentage of the population likes seeing two guys, and they wouldn't do it anyway. Two hot girls going at it is what brings down the house and you know it. It will save a lot of lives, Stacy." Ray stood there giving her the look. The look that he did whenever he wanted something, like a little kid's innocent mug. The front door cracked. She gave in.

"Oh, all right," Stacy turned to Samone who was standing on the couch as if it were mice about to come crashing in. "Are you up for this?"

"I'll do anything," Samone spoke quickly, the tall, beautiful, red-haired singer's wide eyes like a doe in the headlights as she clutched a baseball bat. "Just get me out of here!"

While the others banged against the walls and shouted in the living room, Robby and Clarence slipped out the back bedroom window and made it to the pickup truck. Robby drove the truck around to the back, the others came out one by one through the window and into the bed of the pickup.

Stacy and Samone stood up and hesitatingly began caressing each other and then started French kissing as Robby carefully drove the four-wheel drive pickup up the rutted minibike path. The zombies all followed, bellowing like rutting bull bison when they saw the tall redhead girl and the short blonde going at it. Tony tried to keep both girls upright by sitting and wrapping his arms and legs around both of their legs, still they almost fell out of the truck bed twice. Several fresh rape-ghouls trotted up to the back and sides of the truck but were kicked off by Ray when they tried to climb inside. Robby's skillful driving got them to the summit of the cemetery hill; he drove over some graves and made it to a dirt road that ran down into a little wooded valley with a creek, headstones as far as could be seen in the half-moonlit night. This was the largest cemetery between Saint Louis and Kansas City.

Robby drove them down into the valley of the great cemetery slow enough for the sex zombies to follow. Ray told him to stop at a place by an ornate metal bridge spanning the creek. Stacy and Samone disengaged; Stacy scooped up the HK rifle and then jumped down out of the bed of the pickup. Ray saw by her squinted eyes that she was pissed off and he jumped down after her.

"What's a matter? Did your perfumes clash?" he tried to joke.

"I just didn't like her make-out style," Stacy replied. "So this is it? This is where we make our stand?"

"Yes, this is it. When they come down the hill we'll have a clear field of fire with the side of the valley for a back-stop." Ray looked at her but she didn't look back at him. "What do think, 'Gun-Ho Doc' Masters?"

"I think all these granite headstones will make the little .223 ammo ricochet back at us." Stacy watched the sex zombies coming down the hill in two large, separate groups. About a hundred in each group.

"It looks like all male zombies on the right side and all women zombies coming down the left side of the hill," Robby said.

"It's like a cheesy singles nightclub," Ray said.

"Why don't they just go after each other?" Samone asked.

"Zombies don't do each other," Clarence said. "Don't you ever watch any movies?"

"Maybe it's the smell? The way we move? Who knows?" Ray shrugged and shook his head.

"Let's end this meat-market dance club of the living dead and get out of here," Stacy said. She was still pissed off, Ray could tell.

Ray passed out the ammo to Clarence and Tony. They split into two teams: Stacy and Clarence on the left flank and Ray and Robby on the right. Tony, still unnaturally quiet, seemed to be rebounding after helping Stacy and Samone stay upright in the back of the truck as they escaped from Robby's house. Ray now told him to stay with Samone to guard the pickup. Tony finally got to light up his cigar, pumped a fist salute to Ray and Stacy as he sat puffing away in the back of the truck.

"I know you're not happy about what you had to do back there." Ray got her aside right before the battle was to commence.

"No, that's not what it is, Ray. That was just a joke I'll laugh about. The problem is this whole thing, this whole mess is something I'm always going associate with you. It's a war thing, like in Afghanistan. If somebody gave you bad luck there it didn't matter how nice he was you didn't want anything to do with 'em."

"We make our own luck, Stacy," he said back but she had already turned to walk out to meet the first wave of sex-zombies.

She let Clarence practice shooting the first sex-zombies with the short pump shotgun. Ray and Robby were now shooting their pistols too. When she thought he had mastered the shotgun she said, "Stay behind me off to the side, don't let them get behind me."

Stacy opened up with the HK, precisely putting shots into the genitalia of pant-less onrushing rape-ghouls. The first wave was male zombies and she piled up the bodies. Shooting them made her relationship-jinx angst explode inside her and she started screaming at the zombies: "Look at you!" she shouted to the tenth zombie, "Yours looks like a cocktail weenie; how am I supposed to hit that?" to the next one she shouted, "Yours looks like a moldy pickle!" "How do ya like that, lefty?" she yelled after shooting the next.

After pushing in the fifth clip she heard Clarence shout, "The girl zombies are coming! The girls can't be as bad as the guys!" She turned and watched him run off to meet the onrushing wave of female zombies.

"Get back here, Clarence!" but changing the clip allowed the last male rape-ghouls she was fighting get too close and she had to trick-shoot like Annie Oakley to keep from getting tackled. She heard the shotgun go off three times then too long of a pause and then Clarence was screaming over the banshee-like, orgasmic din of dozens of female sex-zombies piling up on top of him.

"Get off of him!" Stacy charged the pile-up, hitting the gal zombies with the hard composite plastic butt of her futuristic-looking rifle, fearing any shooting would hit Clarence. She made no progress getting them to stop their attack and backed off. Clarence quit screaming. Horrified, Stacy watched a desiccated female ghoul hitch up her mildew covered dress then ram a hand with Clarence's class ring again and again into her vagina. Many other girl-ghouls were now masturbating with Clarence's other body parts. Three were fighting over his head.

"Oh my God," Stacy said. "The girls are worse than the guys; the girls are worse than the guys!" She put a new clip in and proceeded to mow down the girl-ghouls that were now coming for her. After she expended her last rifle clip she pulled out her pistol. She finished the girl-ghouls off, turned to run but Robby was right behind her. The look on his face was grave and without him explaining they made for the pick-up truck were Samone was alone locked inside. Looking seasick, Samone pointed across the bridge. Stacy and Robby got in the truck, Robby turned around to drive across the bridge. She spotted Ray standing near a pile of inanimate male rape-ghouls. Tony's motionless, bloody body was on the ground.

Robby drove the truck right up to them, parked and he and Stacy jumped out of the cab. Stacy ran to Tony's body, she did a quick examination, saw the six gaping open holes in his back and stomach and then the former navy corpsman who had seen several roadside bombings with screaming maimed victims and multiple human body parts in Afghanistan, turned her head and vomited.

"What happened to him?" Robby asked as Samone walked up and hugged his waist, pressing her face against his chest.

"He saw a group of them coming up behind us and ran over here to stop them. When he tried to put in a new clip they got him, about fifteen of them. They chewed holes into him and then sodomized the wounds until he bleed to death. They were still on him, standing him upright when I got here. I pulled them off and blew their nasty asses away."

"This is one sick fucking nightmare." Stacy looked up after finishing retching.

"Hey where's Clarence?" Ray asked.

"He didn't make it," Stacy replied and wiped her mouth. "The shotgun must have jammed. Girl zombies tore him apart and used his pieces for dildos."

When Robby heard that he fainted into Samone's arms, and she struggled to lay him down on the ground. After she did she stood up and pointed at Ray's shoulder. He was bleeding badly.

"Ray, did they bite you? What happened?" Stacy got up fast and went to Ray.

"No, I didn't get bit. One of my bullets ricocheted off of the tombstone over there and nailed me."

"Damn it, Ray why didn't you say something? It looks like it went clean through and missed the bone, but you're losing a lot of blood." Stacy sanitized her hands then dug into her rucksack and pulled out a tampon. She cleaned both entry and exit wounds and then gently pushed the tampon into it then covered both with large gauze.

"Great, now I'm on the rag," Ray quipped.

"No jokes, Ray. We have to get the hell out of here, now. It's done. We finished them." Stacy completed tying a sling around his left arm. She looked up at him with glistening eyes.

"Listen, quiet," Ray said. They did and all around, like the plopping of old snow falling from bare black trees, was the sound of a thousand sex zombies digging themselves out of their graves in the vast cemetery valley.

It was then that Tony's corpse sat up and started moving its arms like it was relearning coordination; the contorted face turned towards the living and then the dead mouth spoke like it was full of marbles: "Why the fuck are your clothes still on?"

Virgin Births

The evangelical atheist
with fire in his eyes
demands I renounce
the Advent, the virgin
birth of Jesus,
at the same time insisting
I proclaim everything
exploded out of nothing
for no reason.

Presidential Smack-Down Round 1

*While awaiting final judgment in Purgatory the deceased, bored ex-presidents
decide to hold a wrestling tournament to find out who is who; all vying for the
title POTUS MAXIMUS. THere can be only one.*

There were four elimination matches
set up for each fifty years
of the American republic.
The first
of the first half of the twentieth Century POTUS
MAXIMUS contests ended fast in a complete surprise.
An enraged, three-
hundred-pound-plus William Howard Taft
jumped off of the top rope corner turnbuckle
and flattened Teddy Roosevelt before the latter
could shout,"Bully!"
After breezing through Calvin Coolidge,
bookworm Woodrow Wilson, Warren Harding,
and a surprisingly game Herbert Hoover, Taft
faced the feisty Harry Truman. He
finally used his weight advantage to pin
Truman's face to the mat, putting the bantam
ex-president's arm in a painful submission hold.
Truman's face had gone cardinal red
when he finally tapped out. The referee
almost disqualified Taft
for not releasing Truman fast enough.
The last match went quicker than any other;
FDR thrown out of the ring
and he lost in the countdown
to get back in.

Dick Nixon with his black Irish moody countenance,

eyes still with that hunted look,
was the surprise in the second half
of the Twentieth Century match-ups, beating
Jack Kennedy to a bloody pulp after both
contestants cheated worse than any of the other
Twentieth Century POTUSes. Next Nixon chased down
the recently deceased
Jimma Carter, who ran around the ring
screaming, "There should never
have been a United States in the first place!"
Carter didn't fight back until he was cornered
and then only slapped wildly until he was swiftly
routed. Carter gave that familiar ashen malaise face
to the booing crowd as he was carried out.
Nixon continued to fight like a madman but lost to Gerald
Ford, the former football hero, who tied him up in knots
and punted him out of the ring.
"You won't have me to kick around any...," Nixon screamed
as he flew,
complete with Doppler effect. The next match with Eisenhower
was a great valorous contest. Ford was the physically stronger
but rather clumsy and Ike
outmaneuvered him. Eisenhower went on
to take out a slightly absent-minded Ronald Reagan
in an almost clean match-up except at the end
Ike pointed behind Reagan and said, "Look Ronny!"
The former actor
looked over his shoulder;
Ike finished him off quickly and mercifully.
The recently deceased Bill Clinton didn't show up,
dodged his call to glory to run off with Jackie O.
and Marilyn Monroe,
taking advantage of JFK's disoriented state. Stately Eisenhower
wasn't ready for the down-and-dirty Lyndon Johnson

who hit so skillfully below the belt the entire male
audience groaned
in unison.
The recently deceased George H. W. Bush sternly
warned "Read my lips; this below-the-belt
aggression will not stand," right before he stepped
into the ring, but when he entered he doubled over
and vomited onto the mat,
collapsed
and surrendered before Johnson could touch him. After
recovering he shouted, "Read
my hips," and jogged out of the ring amid loud jeers.

Presidential Smack-Down Round 2

In an opulent stadium located in the heart of Purgatory, the first semi-final of the POTUS MAXIMUS wrestling contest of deceased ex-presidents has begun!

The River of Memory
flooded over its banks
like the Mississippi in spring
washing me up here,
a muddy old shoe
that can't forget the foot
that wore it,
Lyndon Baines Johnson
marveled to himself as he watched
William Howard Taft dance
around the mat, too much
of an overhanging gut under
the tee shirt that read "TRUST-BUSTER"
for a clear shot at racking the Republican's balls.

I set foot in Washington
without a penny in my pockets,
left D.C. with forty million dollars. That's
the legacy that counts, not the failed
brush-fire war I fed to the Right Wing
or the failed welfare state I fed to the Left.
Certainly not the stolen election of 1960!
They'll never know all I did,
how close I came to indictment
right before Dallas...plausible deniability.

He charged into the rotund Taft,
grappled with sinewy arms.

The match went on and on.
Finally Taft tired and Johnson
got his fingers inside Taft's mouth,
pulled his cheeks apart where
the referee couldn't see.
Panic registered in Taft's eyes,
Johnson delivered unyielding pain
and Taft tapped out desperately.
The Twentieth Century POTUS
championship won but Johnson
felt no victory just a longing
to leap into the River of Forgetfulness
which surprise of surprises
does not exist.

Presidential Smack-Down Round 3

This is political satire. No deceased former American Presidents were harmed during the writing of this piece.

"From the Heart of Purgatory, we now re-join the 19th Century POTUS Maximus wrestling championship!"

Towering, brooding Abraham Lincoln
and the fire-haired
Andrew Jackson battled for hours.
Finally, the gaunt but wiry Jackson grappled
in close and with his file-sharpened teeth
bit off Lincoln's left ear.
Enraged,
Republican Lincoln power-surged
with a ferocious arm twisting,
tearing out Jackson's left arm,
proceeded to beat the Democrat
to the mat
with the bloody end of his own limb.
The referee stopped the match.
The judges, most of whom were
former U.S. Supreme Court judges,
ruled both contenders disqualified.

Amid the ugly chorus
of boos and catcalls that erupted
at the announcement,
Lincoln stood over the imploded
Southerner, pointed the bloody end
of Jackson's arm at the Judges.
"The judges have made their decision,"
Lincoln mocked the Tennessee accent

as he parodied President Jackson's
famous defiant pronouncement
to the Supreme Court, "now let
them enforce it!"

"Look what you did, Lincoln!"
the referee said, pointing
to the unconscious Jackson.
"This is the Afterlife," Lincoln shouted back,
"He'll heal up quick enough."
The 16th American President
strutted across the ring,
raised his arms and Jackson's arm
high like he had been declared the winner
while the audience in the millions chanted,
"Lin-coln! Lin-coln! Lin-coln!"

The judges grew pale
at the audience's exponential anger,
reversed themselves,
and called the match for Lincoln.
Not even bothering
to acknowledge the judges reversal
Lincoln shouted, "Bring that 20th Century
sorry excuse for a Texican out here right now!
Everyone's gonna know
I'm the Top Buck at this watering hole!"

*   *   *

Lyndon Baines Johnson stood
before Abraham Lincoln in the ring
looking as humble as he did
in 1968 after Tet.

"I created the Great Society,
transformed America in the 20th
way more for the better
than you did in the 19th,"
Johnson tried to rabble-rouse.

"Both you and your policies
were about as useful to the country
as a pair of tits on a bull," Lincoln quipped.
He pointed to the words on Johnson's
tee shirt: "'Guns and Butter'! What rot.
Dropping bombs on yellow men
half a world away that hadn't done
anything to the United States. I spent
blood and treasure like nobody before
or since to stop slothful cretins
from living
off the forced labor of other men
and you
turn around a hundred years later
and re-instate it all over again!"

"We do what we must," Johnson said plaintively,
perspiration heavy on his brow.
Oh lordy, he thought. The Lincoln
that stood before him, white streaks
in his brown hair and beard
like Moses
come down from the mountain,
blood-stained bandanna around
his head to bandage his ear,
was not the man from the old photos.
How he died had changed him.
His eyes, his terrible dark penetrating eyes

see everything, communicate every brutal truth.

Not knowing what else to do,
Johnson attacked. Lincoln threw
him to the mat so hard
he went semi-conscious.
Abraham picked him up,
cradled him in his arms
like a son about to be sacrificed,
tossed him up high into the air
spinning like a chicken on a spit.
The Great Emancipator knelt down;
his long gangly knee waited
for Johnson's back which hit
hard, breaking. Johnson gasped,
"We do what we must!" and blacked out.

Presidential Smack-Down Round 4

Epic final round

"...Dejar quisiera
mi verso, como déjà el capitan su espada:
famosa por la mano viril que la blandiera,
no por el doctor oficio del forjador preciada..."
Antonio Machado (from Poem 24)

*   *   *

1828--Lower Mississippi River a few miles upriver of New Orleans.

Nineteen-year-old Abraham Lincoln fell
into a fitful
slumber, blanketed in oppressive Louisiana
mugginess. For many weeks working on a flatboat,
cruising south
with the current
to escape his father
in upcountry Illinois, Abraham
on this day had witnessed his first slave auction.
Black men, women, and children in chains,
being sold out of an enormous stockyard.
Those forlorn and wretched people
deprived of basic dignity, a sight
he would never forget.

Abraham dreamed he was ten again,
a year after his mother's death,
working the farm alone with his sister
and little brother in the Indiana wilderness
twenty miles from anyone.

His father returned
after abandoning them for months
just in time to collect
the money from the meager harvest.
He asked his father
that some of the money
be used to get a doctor
for his ill sister.
His father proceeded to beat hit kick
him to the dirt floor of the cabin,
hollering like a lunatic, "You, Abe
are nothing but a lazy, worthless
scribbler of words, a sneak-reader
of useless books,
with no say in where my money goes.
I own
your work, what little work
you do
and don't you ever forget it!"

Abe awoke in a flash of pain.
His father's enraged wide-eyed
stare became the seething hatred
in a black man's eyes as he
reared back to cudgel Lincoln again
with a hefty hunk of wood.
Abe rose to his full height in fury,
barely out of his bad dream,
and with his flatboat pole
hit his assailant on the chin
so hard his jaw almost came off.
All around shouts and screams
as the gang of escaped slaves
attacked his party. Abe

fought so precisely with his pole,
knocking several others to the ground,
that soon they all ran. Lincoln pursued,
his friend Allen Gentry,
who had also been fighting well,
ran after him, called him back.

"Lincoln, I have never witnessed
the likes of that before. You hear
men bragging about fighting
off a half a dozen men, but it's
all horse shit. This daybreak
on this river bank
I watched you do it!"

"They picked the wrong dawn
to waylay me,"
Lincoln responded,
still in a fighting mood.

"Can't wait to get to New Orleans,
the 'Queen of the South,' get paid
and get in one of them fancy cat-houses
and see what those high-class girls
can do."Gentry smiled, trying to prevent
the onset of melancholy
he saw coming in Lincoln's face.
They started walking back to the flatboat.

"Yes, the sooner we get there the better,"
Lincoln said as he bandaged
his bleeding head with a dirty bandana.

*   *   *

Purgatory--near future.

"...Abe will, Abe will, rock you! Sing it!"
The singer in the checkerboard jumpsuit,
long wavy black hair and overbite
finished the song
in Lincoln's corner and then slid
over to the opposite corner of the fighting ring
to begin the next song,
playing the piano with dramatic gestures. "...George
Washington is the champion of the presidential world..."
After finishing the song, amid thunderous applause the singer
did a cross-legged bow and exited.

The piano was removed and the announcer
entered the ring still clapping.
"Let's hear it again for Freddy!" The roaring crowd
erupted again. "Can't wait for the rest of Queen
to get down here so we can have a reunion concert!
And now, from the Heart of Purgatory,
the Soul of Sheol, the event you've
all been waiting for! The POTUS Maximus
final championship! A clash of Titans!
There can be only one!" The crowd went insane
for the fight as the two contestants entered the ring.
"Hailing from Springfield, Illinois at six feet four inches,
weighing in at one-hundred-ninety-nine pounds,
the Rail-Splitter, the Greeeaat Em-an-ci-pa-tor, Honest Abe
Lincoln!" Crowd roar is deafening.

"And in this corner, hailing from Mount Vernon,
Virginia, at six foot-three inches, weighing in
at two-hundred-ten pounds,
first in war,

first in peace,
and first in the heart of his country-men,
the Father of the most powerful nation in the history
of the globe, General George Washington!"
Crowd roar is again deafening.

George Washington bowed to the announcer
then turned and bowed
to the singer sitting in the front row.
He turned and faced Lincoln.
"You sir, I will not shake hands
with you, a war criminal
that has sullied the name of the United States.
It is always prudent to study
your opponent. Learning how you refused
to see your father after he
called for you on his deathbed
taught me much about you."

"Why don't you tell everyone 'bout my crimes," Lincoln said.
"Spell 'em out, General Blue-Blood. I'm not afraid
to hear every last one of them."

"You wrote pretty words
about 'malice towards none,
charity for all,' while at the exact
same time your army was burning
out of their homes women and children
in villages and cities across South Carolina
in the middle of winter! To their deaths
from starvation and the elements
you sent those helpless innocents!
Your cannons were trained
deliberately on civilian

houses in the great city of Atlanta;
the bodies of women and children,
black and white alike, were stacked up like cordwood.
Instead of court-marshalling them
you promoted your officers who executed mothers
and sweethearts of Confederate guerrillas they could not catch."

"I did what I had to do," Lincoln said.

"You threw out the Constitution,
in order to save it, you claimed.
In every state of the union you
imprisoned without trial
men who spoke out
against you, even pastors!"

"They were nothing but a bunch of trouble-makers,"
Lincoln replied.

"Like some Russian czar despot,
your General Grant signed a military order
forcibly removing Jews from Kentucky and Tennessee."

"Their wheeling and dealing was helping the succesh;
I pretended to be outraged and rescinded it."

"The Crown Jewel of your administration,
your 'Emancipation Proclamation' was not meant to be a new birth of freedom
but rather was designed to incite the negroes outside of your control
to rise up
and slaughter the families of their masters, just as the British incited the negroes
in Haiti to exterminate the entire population of white French there.

It was exactly the same tactic the British tried to do to us during the Revolution."

"We were losing the war in '62; I had to try something outlandish.
The poor whites were rioting and rebelling
in more and more northern cities and back-road counties
because I drafted them but wouldn't draft the rich whites or the blacks.
I sure wouldn't have torn my clothes
if the black slaves down south had rose up
with their cane-cutters and hacked up some lily whites
but it didn't happen. They were too busy singing hymns
to get into heaven to do me any good.
But what I didn't expect did happen.
After the Proclamation the blacks up North, the runaways, started volunteering
and they carried the flag to victory. I was going to send all of them,
free or slave, to Liberia and Central America
after the war but when they started joining up with our cause I
changed my mind. Keeping my own personal army of them to insure everyone else kept in line
was my new plan after old Bobby Lee surrendered."

Washington shook his head. "And now brutal rulers
across the globe,
from Germany to Japan,
to Persia and Syria, the many miscreants
ruling African nations,
all point to your army's example of 'Total War'
on civilians to justify their atrocities!
What have you got to say for yourself?"

"The poetry in my speeches abides,"
Lincoln responded. "The only thing
that never died

on me or went crazy
on me were words in books.
They were my salvation.
The poetry in my words
are the nation's salvation.
If our people go to the stars
or to another Dark Age
they will still have my words
to inspire and comfort them. Despots
will always have Attila the Hun and a hundred other
fiends to blame their 'Total War' on; they
don't need me. But my words abide
and are the salvation
of America and Americans forever."

"Well, it is true
you kept the country from disintegration,
but the hypocrisy in your words is beyond redemption.
I intend to avenge your depredations
on Virginia and Southern people in this ring."
Washington
took off his white gloves and stood
ready for the battle. Despite Washington's
manners and affectations of aristocracy
Lincoln had never come face to face
with a more formidable man, used
to command and physically dominant,
the perfect father figure.

"That sounds good, General Blue-Blood.
Let's quit jawing and get this show on the road!
Like they say
up in the living world nowadays,
'Bring it!'"

Detroit

The Nihilist
in that Russian novel
puts a pistol
to his head
and says,
"I'm going to America,"
pulls the trigger.

I am already in America,
me, Detroit, "The Paris
of the Midwest."
Once I was
the great nursery
of automobile freedom
and motown music;
now I am a bullet hole
in the skull
of a corpse
that keeps walking.

Waiting for the Bird Flu

(With apologies to C.P. Cavafy)

Why are we so transfixed, day and night, in front of the TV?

There have been deaths in a far-away place. Scientists are reporting a Bird Flu pandemic, with 60% mortality, will soon sweep across the entire globe.

Why isn't the U.S. government or the U.N. or E.U. or any other government responding to the crisis? Why are they all silent?

What's the Point? When that Bird Flu virus rages through the countryside it will govern. The virus will decide who to oppress and who gets preferences, decide who will prosper and who will be impoverished, who lives and who dies. Everyone knows the politicians have been out of fresh ideas to deal with our severe, chronic problems for many years anyway; how could anyone think they can handle this?

Why did Al Gore and Leonardo DiCaprio and Bono deplane from their private jets to each give a self-gratifying speech eulogizing all the billions of human beings about die and how hard it is at this somber time to have the responsibilities of a world leader?

Because people waiting to die horrific, drowning-in-your-own-fluid flu deaths like to hear their tributes, their "Candle in the Wind" sung by big-shots before they're bulldozed into a mass grave, not after.

But what is this latest news? The scientists posted out in the Asian jungles are now saying the Bird Flu did not mutate. The deaths were from an endemic disease that turned out to be unrelated to the Bird Flu.

Instead of celebration or at least relief there is widespread consternation and confusion, even anger and unrest. Across the world masses of people spill out into the public squares shouting into the air.

That virus was a kind of solution...

Liver-Eating Johnson Escapes!

1849--What is now the Idaho-Wyoming-Montana border.

Dreaming Moon summoned her son.
Cougar-in-the-Tree
dutifully
stepped into the teepee
out of the snowy night. "Yes Mother."

"You have been chosen to guard
the great white warrior," she said smiling.

"You mean the mountain man
they call 'Liver-Eating Johnson,'
who is said to have murdered
over one hundred Crow
and then ate their livers
like they were animals,
not men. That white man?"
Cougar-in-the-Tree queried.

"Oh, you must not
insult the Whites!"
Dreaming Moon berated him. "His actions
must be put in the proper context.
The Crow murdered his pregnant Salish wife.
You must accept that the Whites
are coming to this country.
They will fill it up and make it
their own, bringing their many marvelous ways!"
"But this is our country, Mother.
This land, these rivers and mountains and plains
belong to our people, the Siksika!"

"That is intolerant!" Dreaming Moon shouted,
"We have been arrogant
people, have attacked and oppressed
so many others we
don't deserve this land."

"But why can't the Whites
stay in their own country?" Cougar-in-the-Tree asked,
"We didn't invite them!"

"It is insulting to even ask that,"
Dreaming Moon continued chiding
her seventeen-year-old son. "We
have so many privileges
just for the color of our skin
the poor Whites could never imagine!
We have the cleanest water,
the best food, so many delicious bison,
rivers swarming with nutritious salmon.
The Whites are stuck in ignorance;
their children are so many
they can't get proper educations.
It would be inhumane to not let as many
as would like to come here. How
could you want to send those poor
Whites back to live in those stinking
cesspool cities of London or New York?
Those places are full of crime and disease!
The sky is so dirty there they die
young because it is too hard
to even breathe!
Your xenophobia should make you
ashamed of yourself, Cougar-in-the-Tree!"

"I am sorry, Mother," he said with bowed head.

"Now go and get to know Mr. Johnson,"
Dreaming Moon said with a sudden smile.
"Ingratiate yourself with him and find out
if he is interested in a new wife.
Tonight I, with some of the other women,
will petition the Chief and Council
to not give this great white man over to the Crow."

*   *   *

Cougar-in-the-Tree
entered the prisoner's teepee.
on the other side of the circular fire-pit
the big white cannibal
sat with his arms tied in front of him
and, behind him, his legs tied
together with a cord attached to his neck.
His great yellow-red beard combined
with piercing blue eyes so different
from the serene eyes of his father,
and Cougar-in-the-Tree
wondered how his mother could be
attracted to such a strange version of a man.
His father had told him years ago
on the day he left her that his mother's spirit
had been captured by dreams
that could never be.

"Water," Liver-Eating Johnson demanded.

"First a question," Cougar-in-the-Tree said.

After studying the young brave for a minute
with his manic, piercing blue eyes
the white cannibal said, "All right."

"Did you greatly love your Salish wife?
Is that why you take vengeance on the Crow?"

"I traded fairly for the Flathead woman,
two good horses and several Sioux scalps.
She belonged to me
and was obedient,
so when the Crow killed her I
began killing the Crow, one hundred and thirty-seven so far.
I have decided that when I have killed three hundred
I will cease and become brother to the Crow again."

"Why do you eat their livers?" Cougar-in-the-Tree
asked with his head down. The white cannibal paused.

"I eat their livers because the Crow believe they cannot
get into the Happy Hunting Grounds without their livers. I eat
their livers to strike terror into their souls."

"My mother is pleading for your life before the Council. She
wants to know
if you are interested in another wife." Cougar-in-the-Tree
paused then went on, "She says that we Siksika
have so many blessings and privileges,
the best food, the best culture, the best
water, and healthy air,
that if we share
it all with you
you will be transformed and we will live
together in harmony."

"Cougar-in-the-Tree,
there is only one real
privilege,"
the white cannibal said with an almost warm smile
through his great blood-soaked beard.
"Forget about wealth or superior culture,
good upbringing or good food,
the one true privilege
is having in your heart the diamond-hard resolve
to do what-ever violence
is required to subdue your personal enemies and the enemies
of your people. Now I would like you to get me some water."

*   *   *

Cougar-in-the-Tree re-entered the Teepee
with a bowl
of melted snow.
As he tipped the bowl to give the prisoner
his drink he noticed too late
the big white man had chewed through
his wrist binding. Liver-Eating Johnson
brought up his great fist in a powerful uppercut
that knocked the young brave semi-conscious.
The white cannibal scooted around to get to
Cougar-in-the-Tree's large knife. He cut himself free
then sawed off the young brave's right leg
at the hip joint,
cut his way out the back of the teepee, and ran
out into the snowy night with the bloody limb.

Other braves heard Cougar-in-the-Tree's
screams.
One tracked the cannibal white man

into the blackness beyond the campfires
only to be stabbed
after turning around in the blinding wind.

Liver-Eating Johnson escaped into the blizzard.
He could not be tracked in the blowing snow,
and subsisting on the raw haunch
of his former guard,
trudged over two-hundred miles into the Rocky Mountains
in the dead of winter without sleeping or making a fire,
made it to his partner Del Que's cabin.

Liver-Eating Johnson is said to have reached his goal
of three hundred Crow
killed, after which he became their brother again.

Later, Liver-Eating Johnson came down out of the mountains
and joined Lincoln's army, went to fight on the Western Front.
Confederate guerillas in Missouri managed to shoot him multiple times
but bushwhacker bullets were no more effective
than the Crow and Blackfoot arrows and spears.
After the war he went back to fighting Indians, mostly Sioux.

Some say he never died
and still lives in the Rocky Mountains
where no one else can go,
always ravenous
for anyone who talks loosely
about their "privilege."

www.ingramcontent.com/pod-product-compliance
Lightning Source LLC
Chambersburg PA
CBHW032150020726
47496CB00003B/802